Amy Cross is the author of more than 100 horror, paranormal, fantasy and thriller novels.

OTHER TITLES
BY AMY CROSS INCLUDE

American Coven
Annie's Room
The Ash House
Asylum
B&B
The Bride of Ashbyrn House
The Camera Man
The Curse of Wetherley House
The Devil, the Witch and the Whore
Devil's Briar
The Dog
Eli's Town
The Farm
The Ghost of Molly Holt
The Ghosts of Lakeforth Hotel
The Girl Who Never Came Back
Haunted
The Haunting of Blackwych Grange
Like Stones on a Crow's Back
The Night Girl
Perfect Little Monsters & Other Stories
Stephen
The Shades
The Soul Auction
Tenderling
Ward Z

MARY

AMY CROSS

This edition
first published by Dark Season Books,
United Kingdom, 2020

ISBN: 9798629969969

Also available in e-book format.

www.amycross.com

AMY CROSS

CONTENTS

AMY CROSS

MARY

AMY CROSS

CHAPTER ONE

November 28th, 1962

IT BEGAN – as it would also end – with a phone call late at night.

Sergeant Ben Warner, sitting at the main desk on his first night in Bilside, reached over and lifted the receiver from the cradle. His shift had only started twenty minutes earlier, and he'd been busying himself by getting acquainted with local cases. Since Bilside was a small town with less than a thousand inhabitants, actual criminal acts were few and far between. Indeed, even a phone call was something of a surprise.

"Bilside Police Station," Ben said into the receiver, "Sergeant Warner speaking, how can I -"

"You have to go and check on her," a worried male voice said on the other end of the line, interrupting immediately. "I need you to make a... what do they call it? A welfare check! I need you to make a welfare check on Mary Moore at Fenford Cottage. Please, it's urgent, I think something might be terribly wrong!"

"Okay," Ben replied cautiously, taking a pen and paper so that he could make notes, "can you start by -"

"Oh, it's terrible," the voice continued, interrupting again. "Something's wrong, I know it. Please, for the love of all that's holy, you have to go and see that she's alright! You have to go right now!"

"Okay," Ben said again, forcing himself to stay calm and focused, "let me start by taking down some details."

"There's no time!" the man insisted, sounding increasingly frantic. "Why won't you just listen to me? You have to go to Fenford Cottage and see if Mary's alright!"

"I will absolutely do that," Ben said, as he spotted his superior, Inspector Lomax, peering through at him from the other room. After a moment, Lomax ducked out of view, but he'd obviously heard some of the conversation. "Let me take down some details," Ben continued, aware now that Lomax was listening and that competence and professionalism were vital. "Can I start with your name, Sir?"

"You have to go!" the man shouted, and now he seemed to be sobbing. "I'm begging you, you have to go and check on Mary Moore! She's at Fenford Cottage, it's about ten miles out of Bilside, you have to hurry!"

"Mary Moore, Fenford Cottage," Ben said, making a note. "Sir, again, can I trouble you for your name?"

He heard a reply, but for a moment the voice sounded garbled, as if the lines were temporarily disrupted. Trying to pick out some kind of detail from the distortion, Ben focused as hard as possible on the twisted, wailing sound that seemed intertwined with some form of static. After a moment, as the receiver itself began to rumble, Ben leaned a little back from the telephone, worried that there was about to be a small explosion. He waited, and the rumbling faded, and then he put his ear to the receiver once more. The static was still strong, but now the voice was emerging from the storm, and could at least be heard properly.

"You have to go out to Fenford Cottage!" the man shouted, his voice twisted with anguish. "You have to check on Mary! Mary Moore! Please, before it's too late, you have -"

Suddenly the call went dead, leaving Ben sitting all alone at the desk and listening to nothing but silence. For a few seconds, not really sure what had actually happened, he kept the receiver close to his ear, before finally lowering it to the cradle. The man's frantic voice still echoed in his mind, and when he looks down at his notepad he realized that he'd really not managed to get many details at all. Had that been his own fault? Or had the man simply been in no fit state to answer questions?

Finally, still a little shaken, Ben picked up the notepad and got to his feet.

CHAPTER TWO

"SIR? WOULD YOU MIND if I... I mean, could I ask you something?"

Standing in the doorway, feeling terribly embarrassed by the fact that he was going to have to ask for advice, Ben watched as Inspector Lomax set down a file and closed the cover. The older man then removed his reading glasses, taking care to set them neatly on the desk, before turning to Ben with a curious, calm expression on his face.

"Well," Ben continues, clutching the notebook as he tried to work out how to explain what had happened, "the thing is, two minutes ago I received a telephone call and, well, I'm not entirely sure what to do about it."

"You're not, eh?" Lomax replied.

"I'm not."

Lomax stared at him for a moment, before sighing.

"Let me guess," he said to Ben with a hint of exhaustion in his voice, "the telephone call was from a man who wanted you to go and perform a welfare check. Is that correct?"

"It is, yes."

"On a Miss Mary Moore?"

"Yes."

"Out at Fenford Cottage?"

"Yes."

"And he was most insistent, I assume?"

"Very."

"Of course he was." Lomax paused, and then he sighed again. "Ben, it's your first night on the job here at Bilside. That's correct, is it not?"

"It is," Ben replied, a little bemused since he knew that Lomax was well aware of the answer to that particular question.

"And I gave you some advice earlier," Lomax continued, "regarding your new role here in the town. You're used to a big city, so coming here must be something of a culture shock."

"I'm awfully glad to be in Bilside," Ben said keenly, "and -"

"I know, I know, you already said that." Lomax sighed yet again. "The thing is, Ben, there are certain things that happen to new recruits around these parts. We don't often have newbies arrive, the last one was Alan Derriford about five years ago. He's a nice man, you'll meet him in a day or two. He has a lovely wife, Doreen, and two smashing kids. Lucy, aged eight, and Michael, aged five. Very popular around town, they are. I'm sure you'll meet them soon enough.."

Ben smiled politely, even though he wasn't sure why he was being given this particular information.

"You ask Alan Derriford," Lomax continued, "or anyone who works here, about their first night at the desk, and they'll tell you the exact same thing. Do you know what that same thing is, Sergeant Warner?"

"No, Sir," Ben replied, before realizing that he should probably come up with a suggestion. "Is it that... strange things happen in small towns?"

"Well," Lomax said with a chuckle, "that might very well be true, but it's not the answer in this particular case. The truth, Sergeant Warner, is that everyone who ever worked here has received that exact same phone call, or a rough approximation of it, on their first night."

Ben waited for him to explain further, but no further explanation was forthcoming.

"The phone call?" he asked finally. "It's... happened before?"

"It happened to me when I started here, and it's happened to every new recruit ever since. A male voice, sounding somewhat harassed and distressed, begging for a check on a woman named Mary Moore at Fenford Cottage. The call is always of a bad quality, indecipherable in places, and the caller seems not to respond to questions. He only repeats his request over and over, usually for a minute or two, before the call ends abruptly. Is that more or less what just happened to you?"

"Well... yes, it is," Ben replied, somewhat shocked to find that the call had precedent. "Are you saying... Should I *not* check on this Mary Moore woman?"

He waited, but Lomax simply stared at him, and Ben began to worry that his question had been foolish. He was so keen to make a good impression, and his mother had warned him to show initiative, and now he wondered whether perhaps he'd missed some nuance of the situation.

"I'm not going to stop you," Lomax said eventually, "if you want to go out there. Others have gone, that's for sure, and they always find the same thing." He paused. "Fenford Cottage is an abandoned little stone place just over ten miles to the south of town. It's an unremarkable place, but it's the only building on that road for quite some distance, so it's impossible to miss. In my time here, half a dozen officers have gone out to carry out this suppose welfare check, and do you know what they've found?"

"What, Sir?"

"Nothing," Lomax continued with a shrug. "I mean, the cottage is there alright, but it's dark and empty and nobody's been there for years. Why, I don't think anyone around here remembers anyone ever living there, and certainly no-one's sure who owns the place now. It's a perfectly nice cottage, it could be done up grand, but the fact remains that there's certainly nobody living there. Mary Moore seems not to exist."

"Well..."

Ben thought for a moment, trying to come up with something sensible to say, something that would impress his superior.

"Well, the address must be wrong, then," he suggested finally. "The caller has some of the details wrong. I'm sure it wouldn't be the first time that somebody got a little muddled. Have you checked to see whether this Miss Moore might be living somewhere else in the area?"

"There's no Miss Moore living anywhere near Bilside."

"Have you tried national registries?"

"I really don't think that's the issue here, Sergeant Warner."

"Have anyone mentioned this to the caller?"

"The caller seems to have no time to listen to suggestions."

"Is it possible that Miss Moore *used* to live

at Fenford Cottage, and the caller was never updated with a change of address?"

Lomax shook his head.

"Well, there must be *some* kind of explanation," Ben said. "I'm sure this fellow wouldn't make this phone call so regularly unless he had a good reason." He paused. "So should I go out there?"

"To Fenford Cottage?"

"The request *was* made."

"As it has been made several times before."

"The caller seemed most convinced that Miss Moore requires assistance," Ben pointed out. "There's nothing else to do, and it would seem like a dereliction of our duty to simply ignore the request."

"Then go," Lomax replied. "See for yourself that there's nobody out there. Don't forget to take a torch, so you can examine the place properly."

Ben opened his mouth to ask whether there had perhaps been some grand misunderstanding, but then he hesitated as he realized that Lomax seemed to be waiting intently for his decision. He told himself that there was no need to go out to the cottage, that by doing so he'd only be making himself look foolish, but then he told himself that he might risk seeming callous and uncaring. Then, he realized, going to the cottage might make it seem as if he didn't trust his superior's judgment. Or would he seem to have no mind of his own, no courage or mettle? He could think of at least ten reasons to go and ten to not go, and finally he realized that with each passing second of silence he risked looking more and more foolish.

"Right," he said finally, "I suppose... I suppose I shall take one of the cars and... go to Fenford Cottage." He paused. "Unless you need me here, that is."

"I can spare you," Lomax replied calmly.

Ben swallowed hard.

"Are you sure about this?" Lomax added.

"I... think so," Ben replied. "I mean, of course. It's absolutely the right thing to do."

"Then off you go," Lomax said. "It might be good for you to head out and see a little of the local area, even if it's a little late now. As you can see, we're not exactly swamped here, so take your time. I just have some reports to finish."

"I won't be too long," Ben said, turning and heading out into the main office, still wondering whether perhaps he'd made the wrong decision. What if he now appeared foolish?

Stopping, he considered changing his mind, but then he realized that this would only cast him as indecisive, which was something he *definitely* didn't want.

"Oh, Ben," Lomax said, "one more thing."

Ben turned to look back over at his superior.

"We traced the call once," Lomax continued. "Every time, it comes from the same house in Belgravia, in London."

"What did the occupants say?" Ben asked. "Were they able to explain what was happening?"

"Perhaps they would have been able to do so," Lomax said, "if there had been any occupants there. As things stand, that particular house has been empty and unused for more than forty years, since well before the war. We established that nobody has been in there for a long time, not even builders or service men."

"That... simply can't be the case," Ben replied, feeling a chill run down his spine.

"That's what everyone else said," Lomax told him, "but an empty building is an empty building nonetheless. And number fifteen, Langford Gardens, is as empty as they get."

"So who makes the calls?" Ben asked.

"Who indeed?" Lomax replied. "Now, if you don't mind, I have some work to get done. These reports won't write themselves, you know."

Ben lingered for a moment, still convinced that he could come up with some kind of answer that would explain everything. Each new possibility, however, died before it could reach his lips, as he realized that the situation felt too strange to truly understand. The only solution, he realized finally, was to grab the bull by the horns and assess things for himself, and there was only one way to achieve that aim. He'd have to go out to Fenford Cottage, and see for himself whether there was any sign of the elusive Mary Moore.

CHAPTER THREE

THE POLICE CAR'S HEADLIGHTS picked out the rugged stone wall of a small bridge, as Ben slowed the vehicle to a crawl on the rough road. The entire car shuddered and jolted as its tires bumped over rocks and dirt, and Ben was starting to feel as if he was out in the middle of nowhere. The headlights illuminated the road ahead well enough, but at the same time they left the surrounding fields shrouded in darkness.

He glanced at his wristwatch.

7pm.

Once he'd safely navigated the car past the bridge, he saw that the road ahead remained rough and pebble-strewn. He'd left the town far behind about half an hour earlier, and now he was starting to doubt that he was on the correct route at all.

Lomax had told him to head south, and there seemed to be only one road heading south from Bilside, but this particular road was getting rougher and narrower as it progressed, to the point that Ben worried it might peter out entirely and lead to nothing but a patch of mud. Had he, he wondered, somehow managed to take a wrong turn, even on a road that supposedly lacked any junctions at all?

He kept his eyes focused on the furthest point that was picked out by the headlights, and finally – after a few more minutes – the road turned and he spotted a long, low metal gate at the side. He slowed the car even further and then brought it to a halt, and then he peered out past the gate. Was there a house out there in the darkness? So far, he could see nothing, but he realized that it behoved him to take a closer look. He kept the engine running, so as to have the headlights as a warning for any other vehicles, as he climbed out of the car into the cold air. After pushing he door shut, he made his way over to the gate and peered out at the yard beyond.

At first, he saw nothing, but after a moment his eyes adjusted to the darkness and he realized he could just about make out the shape of a small, white-walled cottage.

Still not sure that he'd found the right place, Ben hesitated for a few seconds before realizing that he'd have to go closer. He tried to open the gate, although after fumbling for a moment he realized he was at the wrong end. He made his way over and finally located the iron bar, which he pulled aside before pushing the gate open. As he did so, the metal hinges creaked loudly to disturb the scene. The only other sound came from the car, as the engine continued to idle.

After taking care to shut the gate properly, he began to make his way across the yard. The dirt was dry beneath his feet, although his steps still crunched against the ground as he walked closer and closer to the cottage's front door. Already, he could see a wooden sign on the wall, and he squinted slightly in an attempt to make out the words. Then, as he stopped in front of the door, he felt a flicker of anticipation in his chest as he finally managed to read the sign.

Fenford Cottage, albeit with the name barely legible anymore. The sign, clearly, was old and uncared-for.

At least he knew that he was in the right place. Taking a step back, he looked at the pitch-black windows and realized that there certainly seemed to be no sign of life. The garden seemed overgrown and abandoned, and several tiles had long since fallen from the roof and smashed against the ground. All things considered, Fenford Cottage had the appearance of a place that had been left untouched for many, many years, and Ben found it difficult to believe that anyone could possibly have disturbed the site recently. There certainly seemed no prospect of finding a Miss Mary Moore anywhere around.

Still, he had a duty to be thorough, and this was a duty that he intended to discharge.

Stepping over to the front door, he hesitated for a moment before knocking gently. He was already fairly sure that nobody could possibly be inside the cottage, and indeed he was beginning to hope very much that the place was abandoned. He could not really imagine the kind of person who would live in such a place, and – if such a person *did* exist – he was not particularly keen to meet them. Sure enough, after a few seconds, he realized that nobody seemed to be coming to the door, and when he checked his watch again he realized that it was most likely too early for anyone to have retired for the night.

Still...

He knew he should knock a second time, and louder, just to be sure. This he did, rapping the wood with enough force – he supposed – to wake the dead. This time he knew that nobody could miss the sound, not even if they were in bed, perhaps not even if they happened to be asleep. He had knocked loudly and firmly, in a manner that would undoubtedly have pleased his mother; she always criticized him for being too meek and timid, and she'd even hinted that these aspects would hold him back in his work as a police officer, so he was pleased to think that right now he was proving her wrong.

Reaching out, he even tried the door handle, but of course the door was locked.

Look at me now, mother, he thought to himself, *taking charge and dealing with a situation alone*.

Once he was sure that nobody was coming to answer the door, however, he realized that he really had done all that he could. He certainly had no grounds to break the door down, and the cottage simply seemed to have been left locked and abandoned at some point in time. As for the mysterious phone call, he reasoned that he had no means of determining what had caused that strange event, but he told himself that the most important thing was that he'd checked there was nobody in need of help.

He took a step back, but then another possibility occurred to him.

Looking over at the nearest window, he suddenly began to imagine a figure collapsed on the floor. What if Miss Mary Moore *did* require help, but was immobilized or somehow prevented from responding to his knocks? He knew that the possibility was slim, yet he realized that a cursory check would be well within his remit. Even though he was feeling chilly, almost shivering, he took his torch from his pocket and switched it on, and then he made his way to the window and shone the light inside.

Immediately, he found that the light from the bulb actually prevented him seeing anything at all, so he switched the torch off and instead resorted to cupping his hands around his eyes and trying to peer into the cottage's dark interior.

Nothing.

All he saw was darkness.

He waited, hoping that his eyes would adjust and that he would be able to see into the cottage properly, but instead the darkness remained. He waited longer still, convinced that eventually he would at least be able to make out the shapes of furniture, but eventually he had to give up and he took a step back as he realized that the cottage seemed impenetrable. There was moonlight, but this shone on the rear of the building, so after a moment's consideration he decided that he was justified in going around and trying to see into one of the other rooms.

By the time he reached the back garden, he was starting to think that he was wasting time, but at least there the moonlight was strong. Sure enough, when he tried again to look through a window, he found that the cottage's kitchen was bathed in an ethereal blue light that allowed him to see a table set against the far wall, and a couple of chairs, and what appeared to be an old-fashioned stove and counter-top. Once again, the cottage seemed very old and neglected, and Ben told himself that nobody in their right mind would live in such squalor.

The cottage must be empty.

Stepping back onto the grass, he looked at the rear of the building and realized that there was really no point investigating any further. He'd done the right thing by venturing out to Fenford Cottage, of that he was certain, but now it was time to go back to the station and tell Inspector Lomax that he'd discharged his duty to his fullest. It was not, after all, his job to explain the mysteries of the telephone call, since that call had originated from another jurisdiction. What mattered was that he had satisfied himself that no Mary Moore was in residence at the cottage, and that he therefore had no reason to remain.

Turning, he walked back around to the front of the cottage, and then over to the gate. He worried a little that Inspector Lomax would laugh at him for visiting the cottage at all, as if he had somehow failed a first-shift initiation test, but he failed to see how ignoring a call for help could ever be seen as the right thing to do. As he slipped out onto the road and turned to shut the gate, he told himself that at least his own mother would surely approve of his decision. Could he really have been expected to just ignore the call?

And then, as he locked the gate properly, he glanced back toward the cottage and saw a pale face staring out at him from one of the windows.

CHAPTER FOUR

"HELLO?" HE CALLED OUT, hurrying back toward the cottage, keeping his eyes fixed on the spot where the face had momentarily appeared. "Don't be frightened, I only want to help!"

The face – and he was sure it *had* been a face – had slipped out of sight less than a second after he'd seen it, but his heart was racing as he reached window and tried once again to look into the cottage. He cupped his hands around his eyes – again – and leaned closer to the glass – again – and tried to see inside. Still he saw nothing, and then as he took a step back he realized that the face could well be staring out at him still from the darkness.

And it had been a face, of that he was certain.

In his mind's eye, he could still see the pale

features. The face itself had been so very pale, almost completely white, but there had been two dark smudges for eyes and another for a mouth, and a fainted smudge that marked the nose. These features had been framed by unruly hair, such that had made him immediately assume that the face belonged to a woman or a girl, although he knew that this latter assumption was not entirely reliable. He tried telling himself that the face had simply been a trick of the light, that it had not been there at all, but somehow he could not convinced himself of this.

There had, without doubt, been a face at the window.

"Hello?" he said again, still staring at the glass, still wondering what was staring back out at him. "My name is Sergeant Warner, I'm from the police station in Bilside. I'm sorry to disturb you, but I've come to check on a Miss Mary Moore, to see whether she requires assistance. Is Miss Mary Moore here at the cottage?"

He waited, but he didn't really expect an instant reply. Somebody was inside listening, however, of that he was certain, and after a moment he stepped closer to the window again. Reaching out, he touched the glass and found it almost icy, and then he gently tapped.

"You're not in any trouble," he continued, raising his voice slightly even though he was sure he could already be heard clearly. "Would you mind answering the door? I just need to make sure that you're alright."

Again he waited, and again he fully expected there to be no reply. After all, if somebody had chosen to lurk in the darkness and only peer out at the last moment, did it not stand to reason that this person would have no intention now of making their presence known. Quite clearly, they had only allowed themselves to be seen by accident, and most likely now were hoping that they would be left alone.

Yet Sergeant Ben Warner was in no doubt that he had seen someone, and now – as he took another step back from the cottage – he realized that he could not simply turn around and leave.

***

"Inspector Lomax, this is Sergeant Warner out at Fenford Cottage, can you hear me? Uh, over."

He waited again, but he still heard only static from the radio. Sitting in his car, with the engine running, he reached out and adjusted some settings on the radio, hoping that perhaps this would allow him to make contact with the station. He'd been given training on how to use the radio, of course, and at the time he'd assumed that it was a simple piece of kit that even a child could operate.

Now, however, as he sat alone in the car and tried over and over to get in touch with Inspector Lomax, he was beginning to wonder whether the radio was actually working at all.

"Inspector Lomax," he said again, a little more firmly this time, even though he knew enunciation was the least of his problems, "please respond. This is Sergeant Ben Warner, out at Fenford Cottage, requesting assistance and advice. Over."

Again, there was no response, so he tried adjusting the dials once more. The radio should have already been set at the correct frequency, although he had to admit now that he wasn't even sure that 'frequency' was the right word. How did radios work, anyway? Did they automatically switch off at night? So many questions flooded his mind, until finally he leaned back in the seat as he realized that contacting the station in this manner was unlikely to work. He only had two realistic options. Either he had to drive all the way back and speak to Inspector Lomax in person, or he had to use his own initiative and somehow make contact with the inhabitant of Fenford Cottage.

He took a deep breath, before climbing out of the car and then making his way back over to the gate.

***

As he approached the cottage once more, he tried to imagine what Inspector Lomax would do in such a situation. Inspector Lomax struck him as a no-nonsense type of man, as someone who got things done without asking too many questions, and Ben desperately wanted to be the same. Several officers had, over the years, ventured out to Fenford Cottage and – as far as he understood – returned saying that there was nothing to report. Now he, Ben Warner, had an opportunity to rise above them and shock Inspector Lomax by actually returning with news of Miss Mary Moore. In one fell swoop, he could establish himself as a man to be trusted.

He stopped in front of the door. After glancing briefly at the window and wondering whether the pale face was still watching him, he turned and knocked louder than ever.

"I say," he called out, "hello in there! This is Sergeant Warner from the station at Bilside. I'm afraid I must insist that you open this door immediately!"

There.

He'd done it, and he hadn't sounded too bad, either. He'd tried to make himself seem as authoritative and impressive as possible, and he felt he'd done a damn fine job.

Yet, as the second passed and nobody answered the knock, his sense of self-satisfaction began once more to deflate. Whoever was hiding in the cottage, evidently they hadn't been impressed, but he quickly told himself that he simply needed to be *more* forceful, and *more* impressive.

So he knocked again, louder this time. So loud, in fact, that he slightly hurt his knuckles.

"Please open this door immediately!" he said firmly, although he instantly regretted using the word 'please'. He wouldn't again, he told himself. "I'm here on official police business and if you don't answer the door, then I'll be forced to gain entrance other means."

Would he?

Swallowing hard, he realized that he'd rather committed himself now, and that he might end up having to break a window. That thought filled him with dread, although he quickly realized that it was part and parcel of taking charge. He'd never broken a window before, but he supposed that it would be a simple enough task given the preponderance of loose rocks and stones in the garden.

He took another deep breath, and then he knocked again for what he told himself would have to be the final time.

"Now listen here," he called out, "we can have this over and dealt with in just a minute or two, but first you have to open this door. I'm not leaving until I know that anyone in this cottage is alright, do you understand? So open up."

Just to underline that last point, he banged on the door again, and then he took a step back. He checked that his uniform was straight and crease-free, and then he focused on appearing imposing. The occupant of Fenford Cottage was, he assumed, watching him even now from one of the windows, so it was his duty to appear as imposing and formidable as possible. He even tried to puff his chest out a little, in the hope that he could project an image of authority.

And if this failed to work, he told himself, then he would have no choice but to break a window and immediately enter the premises.

CHAPTER FIVE

"THIS IS YOUR LAST chance!" Ben called out, approximately twenty minutes later, as he stood with a rock in his hand and continued to face the window. "I mean it this time. Open the door or I really *will* force my way inside."

He waited, as he had waited before, but the result was no different.

He was being ignored.

How many times had he told the cottage's inhabitant that he was about to break the window? Since picking up the rock and taking his present position, he had phrased the threat in various different ways but it had all amounted to the same thing. Ten, fifteen, maybe twenty times he'd tried to present himself as being somehow important, and he was aware now that this facade was being chipped away with each failed attempt. Now, as he adjusted his grip on the rock and told himself that it was time to take action, he could hear his mother's voice in the back of his head, mocking him.

"You're not a man of action, Ben, are you? You're a follower, never a leader."

Taking a deep breath, he decided that now, finally, he was going to prove her wrong. He mustered all the strength and courage that he possessed, he reminded himself that he was only doing his solemn duty, and then – even surprising himself a little – he managed to throw the rock at the window.

And missed.

Somehow, even from only nine or ten feet out, he sent the rock spinning down against the wall, and then he watched as it landed in the weeds. At the last second, his resolve had failed and he'd let his wrist twist too much, and he'd managed to miss the big, tall, wide window that stood right in front of him. He glanced around, worried that his abject failure had been noticed, and then he scurried over to the weeds and crouched down so that he could retrieve the rock.

Too late, he noticed the stinging nettles.

"Damn it," he muttered, pulling his hand back. After a fraction of a second, he felt the familiar irritating itch on his skin, running from the base of his index finger all the way to the base of his thumb.

Realizing that there were plenty of other rocks around, he grabbed one and then got to his feet again, while telling himself that the figure in the cottage probably hadn't seen what had happened. That was his hope, anyway, as he stepped back and prepared for a second attempt. There was still time to recover the situation and he took yet another deep breath before focusing for a moment and then throwing the rock again.

This time, his aim was perfect.

The rock smashed straight into the window, shattering the glass with such force that Ben actually flinched slightly. He heard the rock thud down against the floor inside the house, and then he waited to see whether or not the inhabitant would react in any way. He half expected to hear somebody screeching and yelling, but after a few seconds he realized that the only sound now came from the car's still-idling engine. He supposed that he should go and switch the engine off, but then he reminded himself that most likely he'd only be another few minutes.

No need to fuss.

Stepping toward the window, he switched his flashlight back on and shone the beam into the cottage's front room. With the glass gone, he could now see several armchairs dotted about the place, although they all seemed to be in slightly unusual positions, mostly facing the walls. The rest of the furniture had all been pushed away from the room's center, and many items such as cups and plates had been knocked off the sideboards and left smashed on the floor. All in all, Ben was struck by the impression that there had perhaps been some kind of physical altercation in the house, and after a moment he even noticed that some of the wallpaper had been scratched away and left hanging.

He leaned forward and shone the light down at the floor, just to make sure that nobody was hiding nearby, and then he shone the light back toward the chairs. He couldn't be certain, but so far it seemed as if the room was empty. Whoever had been at the window earlier, they had apparently scurried off into another part of the house.

"Hello in there!" he called out. "I'm coming in! There's no reason to be afraid, but I need to make sure that you're alright! You can make this easier by making yourself known to me right now. Otherwise, I shall be entering the property forthwith."

Forthwith?

He knew he sounded a little too officious, but then he told himself not to worry too much. After all, it was necessary for him to come across as authoritative and important.

"Alright, then," he continued, realizing that the house's inhabitant was still not willing to play ball, "you're leaving me no choice!"

With that, he pushed some remaining shards of glass out of the window-frame before starting to climb through. Having never been a particularly graceful man, he struggled somewhat even with the business of getting his right leg over the ledge. As he did so, he managed to knock a lamp off the shelf inside, but finally he managed to haul himself into the cottage, at which point he found himself standing on hundreds and hundreds of pieces of broken glass, which crunched loudly underfoot as he took a few steps forward and shone the flashlight all around.

He could see through into the hallway now, although all he saw was floral wallpaper. Of the cottage's inhabitant, there was still no sign.

"Hello there!" he called out again. "I'm inside now, and I think it's high time that you come out and explain yourself to me. Whatever's going on here, I won't be going anywhere until I'm satisfied that the situation is resolved."

He waited.

Silence.

Had he not seen the face at the window, he would now have been more and more certain that the cottage stood empty. He even began to rethink what he'd seen, hoping to find some excuse, some way of perhaps writing the face off as a trick of the light. The more he thought about it, however, the more certain he was that there really had been a pale face peering out at him from the corner of the window, and a moment later he looked down at the spot where the woman – and it had almost certainly been a woman – must have been kneeling.

Aiming his flashlight, he saw several dark spots on the carpet.

He stepped over and crouched down, and sure enough he quickly realized that there were two distinct patches of blood, as if the person at the window had injured knees. Reaching out, he touched the blood with a fingertip and found that it was a little damp, which in turn demonstrated that the blood was fresh. There was a patch of blood on the wall, too, and he couldn't shake the feeling that this third patch resembled the shape of a hand.

Slowly, cautiously, he got to his feet and headed over to the doorway, before stopping and looking out into the hall.

He shone the flashlight's beam both ways, but there was no sign of anyone. There were still some traces of damage, however, and a table near the foot of the stairs had been knocked over. He spotted a door that seemed to lead under the stairs, perhaps to a basement area, and then he noticed some patches of damp that seemed to have spread up across one of the walls.

"I know someone's here!" he called out, and now he was starting to lose his patience just a little.

"I'm a police officer and I insist on you coming to speak to me right now. Don't make me come and find you! I'm here to make sure that you're okay, and that's all!"

Aiming the beam toward the stairs, he watched as banisters' shadow danced against the wallpaper.

"Mary Moore?" he continued. "I'm looking for a Miss Mary Moore. We received a phone call at the station, somebody wanted us to come and check on you. I'm afraid I don't have the gentleman's name, but someone out there is concerned for your health and well-being. Please, just come and speak to me and then hopefully I can be on my way."

The only response, however, was the continued eerie silence of the cottage.

He briefly considered going straight upstairs, before deciding to check the kitchen and other downstairs rooms first. As he made his way across the hall, the floorboards creaked beneath his feet, and he felt certain that this noise was giving away his location in the house. Reaching the kitchen, he shone the flashlight beam around, but there was still no sign of anyone so he turned and went back the other way. Again, the boards creaked loudly, and he felt as if any noise at all represented a kind of intrusion into the peace and quiet of the house. By the time he stopped at the foot of the stairs and shone the beam once again into the front room, he was starting to think that the cottage's inhabitant was clearly far more than just a recluse.

And then, as he turned to go up the stairs, he saw the scratches.

Stepping over to the front door, he aimed the beam at the area around the lock, and to his surprise he realized that there were hundreds – if not thousands – of scratches criss-crossing the wood in all directions. It was as if some sort of wild animal had at some point been furiously attempting to get the door open, and he couldn't help but notice that the keyhole was empty. He tried the handle, finding once again that it was locked, and then he turned to look once again at the stairs.

As he moved his right foot, he felt something crunch and break beneath the soul of his shoe, accompanied by a crackling sound.

Moving his foot aside, he crouched down and took a closer look at some small whitish objects on the floor. Picking one of the objects up, he turned it over in the flashlight's beam, and after a few seconds he realized what he'd found.

Fingernails.

Lots of fingernails.

He gathered the rest up in the palm of his hand. He began to count them, but he soon realized that most of them had been broken into multiple pieces, with blood on some of the edges. Just from a simple visual observation, he felt that there must be a full set of nails, five from one hand and five from another.

Slowly, he looked back up at the scratches around the lock.

CHAPTER SIX

"OKAY, I'M COMING UP," Ben said loudly and firmly as he continued to make his way up the stairs, which creaked loudly beneath his feet. "There's no need to be scared. Whatever's going on, I'm here to help."

As soon as he reached the landing, he looked around and saw three doors, all of which were wide open. He aimed the torch's beam at one of the doors and saw what appeared to be an ordinary bedroom, and the next room looked the same. Wandering over to the third door, he peered inside and found a bathroom. Again, the set-up was noticeably basic and old-fashioned, with just a bath and a toilet plus a sink in the corner. There was certainly nowhere for anyone to hide, so he pulled the door shut and then turned to look toward the other two rooms.

"I know you're here," he said calmly. "What's the point of hiding, eh? Whatever's happened here, I want you to know that it'll all be okay."

Stopping at the door to one of the bedrooms, he shone the beam through and immediately saw a disheveled, unmade and rather dirty double bed. At the same time, he couldn't help but notice a strong fusty smell in the air. He aimed the light at the bed for a moment, before turning to look over at a large, dark wardrobe that stood against the far wall.

"Mary?" he said cautiously, convinced that she had to be close. "It's Sergeant Warner."

Could she be in the wardrobe? Or under the bed? He was starting to realize that there were potentially lots of places where a woman could hide, and a moment later he spotted a hatch in the ceiling that evidently represented the entrance to an attic. He was fairly sure that the woman had retreated upstairs, and that he'd have heard if she's made it back down, so he decided to take a methodical approach to his search.

Stepping back out of the room, he went to the other door and looked into the second, smaller bedroom, where a similarly wrecked single bed stood in the moonlight. There a wardrobe in this room, too, so he walked over and pulled it open to check that nobody was inside, and then he got down onto his hands and knees to look under the bed. There was a lot of debris on the floor, with boxes and other items having apparently been hurriedly shoved down there, but there was clearly nowhere for a person to hide, so he got to his feet.

"So far, so good," he muttered under his breath, as he realized that he'd narrowed things down a little. The missing woman had to be either in the master bedroom, or in the attic.

He walked back through to the other bedroom and stopped for a moment, convinced that he was now closer than ever. Making his way over to the window, he peered out at the road and saw his car still sitting with the engine running, and he began to realize that it really had been a mistake to leave it that way. He'd have to go out there soon enough and at least switch the engine off, but for now he wanted to focus on finding the woman. He looked around, and then he got down on all fours and looked under the bed.

The story was the same.

Somebody had stuffed the space with boxes and books and all sorts of junk, to the extent that there was barely any space at all. He shone the flashlight's beam into the nooks and crannies, lighting up the sides of the boxes, until he was satisfied that there was absolutely nowhere for someone to hide, and then he sighed as he aimed the beam away.

At that moment, he saw a pair of bare feet walk straight past the door, crossing the landing.

Startled, he jumped to his feet and aimed the beam at the door, then he hurried around the bed and ran breathlessly out onto the landing. The feet – and he was sure that he'd really seen them – had been heading toward the other bedroom, so he made his way through there and stopped in the doorway, fully expecting to finally come face to face with the inhabitant of the cottage.

Yet there was no-one.

He shone the flashlight all around, but there was no-one to be seen. There had been no time for the person to hide, and he was certain that this was where they'd been heading, but he couldn't deny now that the room was empty. He checked under the bed again, then he did the same to the wardrobe, but it was as if some person had simply vanished into thin air. That wasn't possible, of course, so he took a step back as he tried to work out what actually *had* happened.

"Hello?" he said, and he was immediately struck by the sense of fear in his voice. Where had that come from? "There's no need to hide. I only want to talk to you."

As he waited in vain for a response, he had to admit that his heart was racing. He'd now glimpsed the cottage's inhabitant twice, first at the window and now in the doorway, so there was absolutely no doubt in his mind that there was somebody nearby. What he couldn't understand, however, was why this person seemed so desperate to avoid being seen. He was certain that he'd done everything right so far, that he'd come across as being firm but fair, yet this person – who he could only assume must be Mary Moore – apparently wanted to stay well out of sight.

Or was he, in fact, the problem?

As he waited for some fresh hint of movement, he began to wonder whether Inspector Lomax would have handled the situation differently. Then again, he reminded himself, Inspector Lomax and all the others had claimed that there was nobody in the cottage to begin with. In that case, Ben reasoned, he'd perhaps already handled the situation better than they had ever managed. He, after all, was the first to actually enter the cottage, and the first to spot somebody moving around. When he imagined himself returning to the station and announcing a resolution to the mystery, he felt emboldened to continue.

He checked another wardrobe.

He checked under the bed.

He checked behind the door.

He opened his mouth to try to reassure the cottage's inhabitant one more time, but then he hesitated. He'd called out already, and he felt certain that she must have heard, in which case he'd only be advertising his presence further. Better, he supposed, to adopt a more stealthy approach, so he turned and headed back to the top of the stairs. As he did so, he was careful to make heavy steps.

"Fine," he said loudly and clearly, "if you don't want help, then I shan't force the matter any further. I'll be going now. I apologize for the window."

With that, he loudly made his way downstairs, and then he stopped for a moment. He had no intention of leaving, of course, but a plan had formed in his mind and he felt that he was being rather clever. He would wait a couple of minutes, so as to give the impression that he'd left, and then he imagined that the inhabitant would emerge from hiding and reveal herself, at which point she'd have no choice but to admit that the jig was up. Accordingly, he walked through to the front room and made a general fuss of stepping across the glass, and then he retreated quietly to an armchair that stood behind the door. Sitting down, he took a deep breath to steady his nerves, and then he began to wait.

The house was silent now.

How long would it take, he wondered, before the woman fell for his ruse? If he was lucky, only a few minutes, although he supposed that things might drag out a little. Still, it was a foolproof plan and he could not imagine how it might ever fail.

And then he remembered the car.

Getting to his feet, he went over to the window and saw his car still sitting by the side of the road, although the engine had cut out. He supposed that, since there was certainly enough petrol in the tank, some feature of the vehicle had simply stopped the engine after a certain time. He briefly considered going and moving the car, but then he told himself that the hidden individual would not be able to see the vehicle until after they'd emerged from hiding. The plan was feeling a little less sturdy now, but he decided that it was still decent, so he quietly went back to the chair and resumed his wait.

Any moment now, he told himself. Any moment.

"I employed the most ingenious ruse," he imagined himself telling Inspector Lomax. "I, and I alone, solved the mystery of Miss Mary Moore at Fenford Cottage. And I did it not through force, but through intelligence."

Yes, everyone would be very impressed.

All he had to do now was wait, and Miss Moore – or whoever was hiding upstairs – would fall right into his trap.

.

CHAPTER SEVEN

ANY MOMENT NOW. Any moment.

Glancing at his wristwatch, Sergeant Ben Warner realized that his wait had now passed the thirty minute mark. The cottage's hidden inhabitant was most certainly proving to be a stubborn opponent, but Ben reminded himself – as he had reminded himself constantly over the past half hour – that she had no way of knowing that he was still around. Wherever she had secreted herself, she couldn't possibly see either him or the car, so eventually she *had* to emerge and reveal her location. Certainly, she was taking longer than anticipated, but that wasn't important in the grand scheme of things.

What mattered was that the plan remained strong.

A few seconds later, finally, Ben looked up at the ceiling as he heard the very faintest of creaking sounds. It was so faint, indeed, that he couldn't even be sure that it had been real, and he wondered whether it had perhaps been caused by the cottage's structure settling in the cold night air. Houses did that, he knew, and the sound – which he fancied had come from somewhere up on the landing – had been too light and too faint for human footfall.

Still, he continued to stare at the ceiling, waiting for the next development.

Which came some two or three minutes later, with another creaking sound that seemed now to be closer to the room directly above where Ben was sitting. That, he told himself, suggested possible movement, as if someone had begun to creep very carefully into the master bedroom. Again, however, he knew that the sound had been so faint as to not possibly have come from a person; no matter how light the woman might be, she would surely have to make more noise. Indeed, he was starting to wonder whether the sound might have been caused by a rat or a mouse. Certainly, a derelict cottage in the middle of nowhere would most likely be home to some wildlife.

Yet the suspicion lingered in his mind that perhaps the woman might be on the move after all. And this suspicion intensified a few seconds later, when another creaking sound came from the middle of the ceiling, indicating that something most certainly was moving very slowly and very quietly across the room above.

Ben almost got to his feet, before reminding himself that he had to wait a little while longer. He was worried about the woman looking outside and seeing his empty car, but he wasn't sure what else he could do. If he made a move now, the woman would most likely hide again, and she seemed most expert at that task. Besides, from what he could tell of the creaking noises, she seemed to be making not for the window at all but for the far side of the bedroom. As far as he could recall, that meant that she was heading toward the wardrobe.

Unless, of course, the noise was being caused by a mouse.

For the next few minutes, Ben sat in silence and waited for another creaking sound. He told himself that patience was a virtue, even as he checked his watch and saw that he'd now been sitting in the chair for a solid forty-five minutes. That was much longer than he'd ever anticipated, but he reasoned that he couldn't abandon the plan now, not after he'd invested so much time. He wasn't quite sure when he'd make a move and rush upstairs, and deep down he was simply hoping that the woman would soon come downstairs, so that he could surprise her out in the open.

"Right, Miss Mary Moore," he imagined himself saying, "what's all this about, eh? You've been sneaking about ever since I got here, and I fancy that means you're up to something. How about you start by telling me about those fingernails you left on the floor?"

She'd have to tell him the truth. Perhaps she'd resist at first, but he was sure that eventually she'd have no option but to reveal everything. As a fairly regular and straightforward sort of person, Ben Warner didn't have much time for people who were 'strange', and by now he was very sure that Mary Moore was not like most people. Evidently she didn't want to be found, and he felt naturally suspicious of anyone who preferred to avoid an officer of the law. Why, she might even -

Suddenly the ceiling creaked again, louder this time, and Ben instinctively got to his feet. The armchair groaned as it lost his weight, though not loudly enough to alert anyone.

Staring once more at the ceiling, Ben realized that this time there definitely seemed to be somebody in the master bedroom. Whereas the earlier sounds had been barely audible, this been clear and distinct, and he was absolutely convinced that it had been caused by a single, firm footstep. Whoever was up there, evidently they had begun to get a little more confident, which in turn meant that they might be about to make a mistake.

As much as he wanted to rush back up, therefore, Ben forced himself to stay in the middle of the living room and wait until he heard footsteps on the stairs.

Any minute now.

She *had* to break.

A moment later, he heard the undeniable sound of another footsteps. Someone was definitely walking across the master bedroom.

Soon they'd come downstairs.

They had to.

And then, slowly, there came another noise. A kind of creaking, but more sustained, as if a door somewhere upstairs was being teased open and its hinges were desperately in need of oil. As if -

Suddenly a loud, anguished scream filled the house, ringing out from upstairs.

Startled, Ben stood completely motionless for a few seconds, but the scream continued. Finally, rushing through to the hallway and then hurrying upstairs, he scrambled to the landing and ran into the front room. Just as he did so, however, he heard a heavy thudding sound and the scream came to an end.

Stopping in the doorway, Ben looked through into a completely empty room.

His heart was racing, and he knew this wasn't possible, but there was no sign of anyone. He rushed out and checked the other rooms, just in case he'd somehow been wrong about the location of the scream, but by the time he got back to the master bedroom he was more certain than ever. Somebody in *this* room had let out an ear-piercing scream of terror, a cry that had seemed to momentarily shake the entire house, and this person could not simply have disappeared into thin air. Nevertheless, that was exactly what seemed to have happened, and Ben began to wonder whether he might be losing his mind.

Until, finally, he realized he could hear somebody sobbing in the wardrobe.

"Hello?" he said cautiously, before starting to make his way over. "It's okay, I'm here to help."

A moment later his right foot pressed against a loose floorboard, causing a creaking sound. This board, he was sure, he had heard while he was downstairs.

The sobbing continued.

"Don't be afraid," he continued, getting closer to the wardrobe and finally reaching out toward the handle. "I'm not going to hurt you, I only want to -"

Suddenly he heard a bumping sound over his shoulder. Turning, he saw that the door to the room had swung fully open and had nudged the wall. He watched for a moment, as the door came to a stop, and then he turned to the wardrobe again.

"My name is Sergeant Ben Warner," he said,

even though he knew he'd already announced his name several time since arriving at the cottage, "and I'm going to make sure that you're alright."

He started to open the wardrobe door, only for something to pull it shut again. When he tried the handle for a second time, he found that somebody was holding the door firmly from the inside. He knew he could use force, but he still wanted to win the trust of whoever was on the door's other side.

"Why are you so scared?" he asked. "Please, I'm a police officer, I only want to make sure that you're alright."

He tried the door again, but the sobbing intensified and he quickly realized that he'd have to use brute strength. As the sobbing continued to get louder and more frantic, he finally grabbed the edge of the wardrobe's door and forced it wide open.

CHAPTER EIGHT

"NO!" THE WOMAN SCREAMED, lunging at him and grabbing the door, pulling it shut so fast that he barely got his fingers out of the way. "Leave me alone! Get out!"

Startled, Ben stared at the door for a moment before trying again. He managed to pull the door open enough to allow him to slide his fingers into the gap, and this time he was better prepared. Even as the woman desperately attempted to stop him, he pulled the door all the way open, and then he watched with shock as the woman tumbled out and landed in a sobbing, screaming mess at his feet.

"Get out!" she shouted as she stood up. "Get out right now!"

"Are you Mary Moore?" he asked.

"Leave!"

Shoving him hard in the chest, she sent him stumbling back, and then she tried to climb once more into the wardrobe. Quickly regaining his balance, Ben grabbed the wardrobe door again and used his body weight to keep it open. The woman tried to stop him, but she lacked the strength and finally she clambered back into the wardrobe and stared out at him with wide, terrified eyes.

"You have to go!" she sobbed, as tears streamed down her face. "Now!"

"I'm not leaving until I know what's going on here," Ben replied, still stunned by the woman's appearance. She was utterly disheveled, with stringy black hair, and there were cuts and bruises all over her face and neck. Her white dress was stained and torn, and a foul smell lingered in the air. "Let's just calm down and start at the beginning," he continued. "Can you confirm your name for me?"

"You don't understand," she whimpered, "it's not safe for you to be here."

"Are you Mary Moore?"

"You have to leave. Why are you here? You have to get out while you still can."

"Are you here alone?" he asked. "Just, please, at least tell me your name."

"Get out!" she shrieked.

Realizing that he was having little success, Ben tried to think of a better approach. He'd always found women difficult to deal with, especially emotional women, which he found surprising given that he'd been raised an only child by his mother. This particular woman before him now, cowering terrified in the wardrobe, seemed so frantic and so deranged that he had no idea how to get through to her. Indeed, he was rapidly coming to the conclusion that she must be mad.

"Please try to realize," he said cautiously, "that I cannot simply leave you here while you're in this condition. We received a telephone call this evening at the station, asking us to come and check on a Miss Mary Moore at this address. Can you start by confirming your name, please? Are you Mary Moore?"

"You have to get out before it's too late," she sobbed. "You don't have much time! If you wait too long, she won't let you go!"

"I don't -"

"Get away from him!" she screamed suddenly, looking past Ben. "Go away! Leave us both alone!"

Turning, Ben saw only the empty room and – further off – the open door that led out onto the hallway. He waited a moment, in case there was any sign of movement, but then he reminded himself that there couldn't possibly be anybody else in the house.

"I know what you want!" the woman cried as Ben turned back to look at her. "Please, just let it end!"

"Who are you talking to?" he asked.

Instead of answering, she dissolved into a series of deep, retching sobs that caused her whole body to shudder. With her face in her hands, she seemed after a moment to be muttering something to herself, but the words were lost in her heaving cries.

Again, Ben looked back across the room. He was convinced now that the woman must surely be out of her mind, and he was trying to determine how best to handle the situation. He was starting to think that perhaps he should go back out to the car and try the radio. He'd been unable to get in touch with the station earlier, but he desperately needed advice from Inspector Lomax.

Turning back to the woman, he saw that she was still weeping uncontrollably.

"I want you to come with me," he said finally, reaching a hand out toward her. "Can you do that? You're not in any trouble, but I can't in good conscience leave you here in this condition. Please, you have to come with me."

He waited. When she failed to respond, he reached into the wardrobe and took hold of her left arm just below the wrist, hoping to tease her out of the wardrobe.

"There's nothing to be frightened of," he told her, trying to sound calm and reassuring. He pulled very gently on her cold, sweaty arm, but found that she was resisting. "Let's just at least get you out of the wardrobe, shall we? I'm sure things will start to feel much better if you're, say, sitting on the edge of the bed, or perhaps in that chair by the window."

"You don't understand!" she said, suddenly looking up at him with tear-filled eyes. "She won't let me leave! She's never let me leave!"

"And who is *she*, exactly?" he asked.

Seemingly unable to reply, the woman simply continued to cry, as her bottom lip began to tremble. Having never before seen anyone in such a terrible state, Ben felt momentarily lost for words, and he certainly had no desire to forcibly remove the woman from the wardrobe. Finally, unable to come up with any better idea, he let go of her arm and stepped back, and then he sat on the end of the bed. As he did so, he briefly spotted himself reflected in the bedroom window.

"What are you doing?" the woman sobbed.

"I'm not leaving without you."

"You have to! You've got to go right now!"

"Then come with me."

"I can't!"

"Why not?"

"Because she won't let me!"

"You keep referring to somebody else," he replied, hoping to reason with her, "but there's nobody else here, is there?" He paused, and he was starting to think that perhaps he was making some headway. "I've been all through the house, Mary," he added. "You *are* Mary, aren't you?"

The woman hesitated, and then slowly she nodded.

"I've checked the place out," he explained, "and you and I are the only ones here. Now, how about you tell me why you were trying to avoid me? Why did you climb into the wardrobe when I arrived?"

"I didn't," she stammered.

"I know you did, Mary."

"I was already in here," she continued. "I've been in here for... days. Two days, I think."

"That's not true," he replied, trying to stay calm. "It's not good to lie to a police officer. You know that, don't you?"

As he waited for an answer, he happened to look down at her feet, and he saw that she was wearing a pair of tattered black socks. He'd spotted bare feet walking past a doorway earlier, but he supposed that Mary had for some reason put the socks on when she climbed into the wardrobe. That made very little sense, of course, but then he was increasingly certain that he was dealing with a strange case. A case, indeed, for which he felt very much ill-prepared.

"You were sneaking around," he continued,

"trying to avoid me."

She shook her head furiously.

"I heard you, Mary."

"That wasn't me!" she spluttered.

"I heard you creeping across this very room."

"That wasn't me!" she yelled. "It was her! I was hiding in here and I could hear her coming closer and closer and then she tried to open the door. She wanted to get to me. She was here, and then suddenly she stopped, when you came up! She wanted to get to me again!"

Ben opened his mouth to remind her yet again that there was nobody else in the house, but then he sighed. Being calm and rational seemed, so far, to not be working very well at all.

"She's right behind you," Mary whispered suddenly.

"I'm sorry?" he replied.

"She... She's right behind you. Don't look at her."

He waited for her to explain further, but then he realized that Mary wasn't actually looking at him. Instead, she seemed to be looking at something over his shoulder. He began to smile, but then he hesitated as he realized he could see a kind of frozen terror in Mary's face. Obviously there was nobody behind him, he knew that, but he was unnerved by the realization that Mary certainly seemed to believe what she was saying. The longer he looked into her eyes, the more he found himself wondering what she thought she could see.

Finally, supposing that he had to break the tension, he turned to look for himself.

"No!" Mary screamed. "Don't!"

CHAPTER NINE

NOTHING.

"Nothing," he said, with a flicker of relief as he looked back across the room and saw only the empty bed, and the door beyond.

He waited a moment, just so that Mary would realize that he'd looked properly, and then he turned back to look at her again.

"See?" he continued. "There's -"

Suddenly he spotted his reflection in the window, except this time there was another figure too. For a fraction of a second, he stared in horror at the reflected sight of an old, haggard woman standing right behind his shoulder. Time seemed to freeze all around him as he watched the woman, and then he saw her right hand slowly reaching out to touch him.

Stumbling to his feet, he spun around, only to see that there was still no sign of anyone behind him. Then he looked at the window again, but this time he saw only his own reflection. The strange woman was gone, yet just a moment earlier he had seen her as clearly as anything.

Slowly, he turned to look back into the wardrobe.

Mary was staring at him.

He opened his mouth to tell her that everything would be alright, but then he looked at the window yet again, concerned that the strange woman might appear again at any moment. There was no sign of her now, but he couldn't help looking all around.

"You saw her," Mary said.

He turned to her.

"You did," she continued. "It's in your eyes."

"I saw no such thing," he stammered, although he was painfully aware that he sounded less than convincing. "I just... I, uh, I mean, I look and I..."

He paused.

"I..."

"It's too late once you've seen her," she told him, and now her frantic panic seemed to have faded a little, replaced by a kind of calm. Or was it acceptance? "I'm so sorry. I tried to warn you."

He paused, and then – feeling as if he'd humored Mary for long enough – he got to his feet. He was feeling a little panicked, and he couldn't help glancing yet again at the window. He wanted to reassure himself that the strange woman had never been there in the first place, and then – as he turned back to look at Mary – he realized that it was time to get out of the cottage.

"We're leaving," he said firmly. "Now."

"We can't," she replied softly.

"I'm sorry," he said, aware of the tremor in his own voice, "but I'm a police officer and I'm taking charge of this situation. I'm ordering you, right now, to get out of that wardrobe and come with me immediately."

"You just don't get understand."

"Get out of there!" he said, almost shouting. "Immediately!"

Instead of obeying his order, Mary actually pulled back a little further into the wardrobe, as if the thought of emerging was simply too much. A moment later she managed to pull back even deeper into the wardrobe, until only her legs were visible.

"I don't know what's happening here," Ben told her, struggling to contain his frustration, "but I *do* know that I'm going to get you out of this place, and then we'll begin to work it all out. Miss Moore, I've been very patient with you thus far, but you really have to cooperate now. If you don't get out of that wardrobe immediately, I might very well be forced to come in there and get you!"

He waited.

She made no move to obey.

Realizing that actually dragging the woman out would be impossible, he sighed as he tried to come up with a better idea. At the same time, he couldn't help glancing over at the window, just to reassure himself once again that there was absolutely no sign of the strange woman. No matter how many times he told himself that she'd hadn't actually been there at all, he couldn't get rid of a niggling doubt in the back of his mind, and he was starting to think that something about the house was starting to get under his skin.

He needed to get some fresh air.

"If you don't come with me right now," he stammered, "then I'll... I'll leave you behind."

He instantly regretted this threat, since he knew it sounded hollow. Still, it was a measure of his utter desperation, and after a moment he stepped forward and leaned fully into the wardrobe. He could just about make out Mary's terrified expression, and of course the foul smell was more pungent in such an enclosed environment. For a few seconds, struggling to work out what to say next, Ben simply stared at her and hoped that she'd snap out of her strange behavior.

"What are you so afraid of?" he asked

finally.

"She's out there," Mary sobbed.

"Can you just focus for a moment and explain this whole situation," he continued. "There's obviously nobody else here, but who do you *think* might be after you?"

"You saw her," Mary replied.

"No, I -"

"You did!" she snapped angrily. "I saw it in your eyes and now it's too late! Once you see her, there's no way out, you're trapped in this house forever!"

"That's patently absurd," he replied.

"I was trying to get to the attic," she continued. "That's the only place she never goes, I hide out there sometimes, but I came down a few days ago because I needed..." Her voice trailed off for a moment, as if she was lost in some terrible memory. "I always end up coming down," she added finally. "I can't stay up there forever, even though it's the only safe place. She leaves me alone when I'm up there, although I still hear her. Sometimes I look down through the cracks and I see her, and she sees me. That face... she looks so furious."

"What exactly do you think will happen if you come out of the wardrobe?" he asked.

"She'll be cautious around you," she replied, "at least at first. I think so, anyway. That's why she's staying back. I don't quite understand, but it won't last forever. Soon she'll come for us both!"

Staring at Mary, Ben realized that while she might be babbling incoherent nonsense, she certainly seemed to *believe* what she was saying. Her fear was genuine, and he had no idea how to get through to her and make her realize that she had to leave. Inspector Lomax, of course, would know exactly what to do, and for a moment Ben felt utterly inadequate. Then, realizing that he was starting to feel sorry for himself, he decided that he'd have to try another tactic.

"Tell me about her," he said. "Tell me -"

"She's coming!" Mary screamed, suddenly pointing past him.

Turning, Ben expected to see only the empty room. Instead, he felt his heart skip a beat as he saw a figure standing out on the landing. Barely visible, more like a smudge in the air, this figure had the shape of the woman from the reflection, and Ben took a step back as he saw two ghostly, pitiless eyes glaring straight at him.

CHAPTER TEN

AFTER SIGNING THE FINAL report of the evening, Inspector Alan Lomax slipped the lid back onto his pen and leaned back in his chair, and then he looked over at the clock on the far wall of his office.

Five minutes to midnight.

Betty would be expecting him at home. He'd told his wife that he might have to work late, on account of having a new recruit in the office, and of course she'd been very understanding. Betty knew that the life of a police officer was rarely simple, and she'd promised to have a nice dinner ready to heat up in the oven. Lomax was starving, and all he wanted to do was get home to his wife and then retire to bed, but as he looked over at the doorway he couldn't help but wonder about Ben Warner.

Where was the young man now?

Several hours had passed since Sergeant Warner had headed off to Fenford Cottage. Lomax had almost told him not to bother going, but then he'd supposed that he shouldn't deny the chap his rite of passage. Still, he should have been back at least one hour earlier, and Lomax couldn't help but wonder what could have caused the delay. Getting to his feet, he wandered across the office and peered out at the parking area at the front of the station, but the second patrol car was still absent.

"Where are you?" he muttered under his breath.

The only likely explanation, barring an accident, was that Warner had simply headed home after visiting Fenford Cottage, but that supposition didn't sit entirely right with Lomax. He didn't know Warner too well, of course, but he believed the young man to be very conscientious, so the idea of him having simply driven home – against all the rules of the station – was impossible to believe. If there had been an accident, Lomax was almost certainly have heard by this point, and he knew that there was no way Warner could still be at the cottage. So the question remained.

Where was he?

Sighing, Lomax went out into the main room and approached the radio. He checked that the dials were in the correct position, and then he attempted to make contact.

"Bilside to car two," he said, hoping to receive a response, "come in. Car two, what is your position? Over."

He waited, but all he heard was static. The radio was usually pretty reliable, although he knew there was a chance that the new recruit might have messed with the buttons. Still, something didn't feel right, and Lomax was reluctant to go home until he knew what was happening.

"This is Bilside, calling car two," he said, trying the radio for a second time. "Sergeant Warner, can you hear me? Over."

Again, the only response was static, and Lomax slowly lowered the radio as he tried to work out what to do next. Driving out to Fenford Cottage felt rather excessive, and he told himself that he could absolutely trust young Ben Warner. Still, something was stirring in the pit of his stomach, a kind of fear that he simply couldn't dispel. By letting Warner go out to the cottage, had he made a terrible mistake?

***

"Did you enjoy your pie, dear?" Betty asked as she shuffled through from the kitchen. "I hope it was warm enough."

"As perfect as ever," Lomax replied with a

smile. "I'm sorry I only ate a few mouthfuls, though. I just have a lot on my mind."

"Something to do with work?"

"Something like that."

She took the plate and limped back to the doorway, before stopping and turning to him. She hesitated, clearly concerned. After forty years of marriage, she'd learned to read her husband pretty well, and she could tell whenever there was something on his mind. Most of the time he seemed fairly relaxed, but there were times when he quite clearly brought his work home. This was one of those times.

"You had a new lad with you this evening, didn't you?" she said finally. "I didn't imagine that, did I?"

"You did not, no," he replied.

"And how was he?"

"Fine," Lomax replied. "I think."

"You think?"

"It's nothing," he continued. "His name's Ben Warner, and he shows every sign of becoming a valuable member of the local community. He comes highly recommended and I honestly think that he's going to be a great asset."

He paused, and now all he could think about was the image of Ben Warner stepping out of a patrol car and making his way toward the darkness of Fenford Cottage. In his mind's eye, he saw the cottage's windows, and he thought back to his own first night on the job, when he – as a young man, all those years ago now – had gone out there to check on the mysterious Mary Moore. He remembered those dark, unforgiving windows that refused any glimpse of the cottage's interior.

"So what's troubling you?" Betty asked.

"Nothing."

"Don't try to pull the wool over my eyes, Alan Lomax," she replied. "There's some part of this rigmarole that you're not telling me."

"Honestly, it's nothing," he said, trying but failing to offer a reassuring smile. "I suppose I just worry, that's all. I feel as if these new recruits are always like little birds, under my wing, and I want to make sure that they're alright." He paused. "I never specifically told Warner that he had to bring the car back. His shift ended a few hours ago, so it's perfectly possible that he just drove home. It's probably my fault for not being clearer."

"What are you on about?" she asked.

"Nothing," he replied, shaking his head. "You know what I'm like, I'm just fussing."

"Will you be able to sleep tonight?"

"Of course," he said, again trying his best to seem relaxed. "You go up, and I won't be long. I just need to sit and think for a few minutes. It's been a long day."

He tried to make his smile look as genuine

as possible. As Betty left the room, however, the smile quickly faded, and Lomax felt himself once again thinking about Warner at the cottage. He still desperately wanted to believe that everything was alright, yet he couldn't quite convince himself that this was true. Of course, he'd let new recruits go out to Fenford Cottage before, and they'd always come back fairly quickly with nothing to report. The whole thing had become a kind of ritual, almost a grim joke, but this was the first time anything had seemed to go awry. And as he sat alone at the dining table, Alan Lomax couldn't help but think back once more to his own visit to Fenford Cottage, to the one thing he'd seen that night that had chilled his bones.

Finally, unable to stop himself, he got to his feet and hurried through to the hallway.

"I'm just popping out to check on something, Betty!" he shouted as he opened the front door. "I shan't be long!"

CHAPTER ELEVEN

"SHUT THE DOOR!" MARY screamed. "Hurry! Shut it!"

After a moment's hesitation, during which he could only stare in horror at the woman on the landing, Ben finally sprang into action. Hurrying across the room, he reached the other side just as the ghostly figure took a step forward. With his heart pounding in his chest, Ben slammed the door shut, and then he turned the key that had been left in the keyhole just below the handle.

"Who was that?" he whispered, stepping back, already doubting what he'd seen now that the door was shut. "She looked..."

His voice trailed off.

Suddenly hearing a bumping sound, he turned just in time to see Mary clambering – at last

– out of the wardrobe. After spending so long inside the contraption, she now seemed to be bursting with energy, and she immediately climbed up onto the bed and reached up for the hatch in the ceiling.

"Come on!" she hissed. "It's the only safe place!"

"We have to get out of the -"

"She won't let you!" she said firmly, struggling to reach the handle. She had to resort to bouncing slightly on the bed. "She'll get through that door soon, and then it'll be too late! We have to get up into the attic while there's still time!"

Looking down at her hands, he saw that her fingernails were all gone. The tips of her fingers were red and bloodied, but also worn, as if they'd been hurt long ago.

Lost for words, Ben turned and looked back over at the door, only to freeze as he saw that the key was jiggling slightly. He told himself that this was just caused by Mary still bouncing on the bed, but a moment later he watched with growing horror as the key very slowly began to turn. Still, a few more seconds passed before he was able to accept what was happening, and then he turned to see that Mary was still struggling to get the hatch open.

"Let me!" he stammered, climbing up onto the bed and quickly grabbing the handle.

"You go first!" she told him.

"Absolutely not," he replied. "Use me for

support. Get up there."

Without waiting for her to argue, he grabbed Mary by the waist and hoisted her up. She quickly grabbed the edges of the open hatch, and then Ben pushed her legs and helped her to wriggle up and out of sight. Then, reaching up, he prepared to haul himself after her, only to freeze at the last moment as he heard the door slam open behind him. In an instant, he felt the hairs start to stand on the back of his neck, and the temperature in the room seemed to drop by several degrees.

Slowly, still hoping against hope that none of this was really happening, he turned and saw the ghostly figure standing in the doorway.

Now, for the first time, he was able to make out her features properly. She had the face of an old woman, withered and lined. Her lips were black, perhaps showing signs of decay, but it was her eyes that spoke most keenly of death. Sunken and withdrawn, discolored and slightly gray, they seemed to have moved back a little into the hollows of her eye sockets, forcing the skin all around to cling much more firmly to her cheekbones. Her skin was pale, and her grayish-black hair hung down over her shoulders. She was wearing a dark, undecorated dress that covered all of her body save for her head and her bony hands.

She took a step toward him.

Suddenly startled and realizing that he had

to get away, Ben turned and reached up again for the side of the hatch, only to slip and fall. He landed against the side of the bed, and then he tumbled over the edge and hit the floor. Winded slightly, he stumbled to his feet, and then he turned to see that the woman had made her way closer. His first instinct was to try again to get up into the attic, but then he realized that the woman would be able to reach him, so he backed away into the corner.

"Hurry!" Mary yelled from the attic. "Don't let her get to you!"

Again, Ben tried to work out a way to reach the attic, but again he could see that the ghostly woman would easily get to him. She was effectively blocking his route to the door, too, and for a moment he could only stand in the corner of the room and try to come up with some kind of plan.

"I'm an officer of the law," he stammered finally, not even realizing that he'd been going to say anything, "and I... I command you to... back away immediately..."

Even as those words left his lips, he knew how foolish they sounded. His muscles momentarily tensed as he considered trying to rush past the woman, but then fear held him back. For a few seconds, as she took another slow step toward him and raised her hands to reach out, he felt as if there was nothing else he could do. He watched her hands reaching toward his face, and he felt his cheeks starting to chill as the air began to freeze.

"Over here!" a voice yelled suddenly, and Ben saw to his shock that Mary had jumped back down from the attic and had landed on the bed. She was already scrambling to her feet and hurrying to the door. "It's me you want, isn't it?" she continued. "Come and get me!"

The ghostly woman turned and looked at her, and then she let out an angry snarl as she started heading back across the room.

"Get up there!" Mary said firmly to Ben. "You know what to do! Do it now!"

"But you -"

"Don't worry about me!" she continued, stepping backward out of the room as the ghostly figure advanced toward her. "I've lasted this long, I've still got a few tricks up my sleeve!"

With that, she turned and hurried out of view, closely followed by the woman. Ben watched in horror as they both disappeared from view. A moment later, he heard a creaking sound coming from the other room.

"I need to know that you're in the attic!" Mary shouted after a few seconds, from somewhere far off in the house. "Don't complicate this! I'll be fine, but you have to trust me! Get up there!"

Ben hesitated, convinced that he should go and help her, but then he realized that she seemed to know far more than him about the situation. He felt that, as a police officer, he should go and take charge, but he was terrified by the thought of seeing the woman again. Stepping over to the bed, he looked up at the attic hatch, yet something held him back. Climbing up there would be cowardly, and he had sworn to himself – many years ago – that he would never shirk from his responsibilities.

Despite Mary's warnings, he began to make his way toward the door, even as fear gripped his chest.

"Hey!" a voice yelled behind him, and he turned to see that – somehow – Mary was back in the attic hatch again. "Seriously? Get your bum up here!"

Startled, Ben looked out onto the landing again, just as the woman emerged from the other bedroom and snarled at him. This time, filled with absolute panic, he moved much more quickly. Climbing up onto the bed, he reached up and grabbed the edges of the hatch, and then – with Mary helping – he managed to pull himself up. After a moment he became stuck, and he had to start lifting himself again, until finally he was able to roll onto the floor of the attic.

He turned and looked back down, just as the ghostly woman stopped beneath the hatch and looked up. She stared at him with fury in her eyes, then she screamed, and then Mary slammed the hatch shut.

CHAPTER TWELVE

AS HE EASED THE car around the corner, Inspector Alan Lomax felt a flicker of fear in his chest. His vehicle's headlights picked out the stone wall that ran alongside the road, but more ominously they also picked out the second patrol car that Ben Warner had taken earlier in the evening. That car was parked at the side of the road with the lights off. As Lomax brought his own car to a halt and switched off the engine, he knew that the presence of the other car could only mean one thing.

Ben Warner was still at Fenford Cottage.

But why?

There was nothing there, at least nothing of note. Lomax told himself these simple facts over and over again, trying to make himself believe that there was no reason to worry. Still, he couldn't imagine what might have kept Warner at the location for over four hours, and it was already clear that the other car was empty. As he sat in darkness and peered out at the pitch-black cottage, Lomax focused on the fact that Warner would have had no reason to actually enter the cottage, since the place was demonstrably empty. And yet...

And yet, as he felt his chest tighten with fear, Lomax allowed himself to think back to the only other time he'd ever visited Fenford Cottage, and he allowed himself to remember something he'd tried so hard to bury in the deepest recesses of his mind.

He'd been a young man back then, roughly Warner's age. When the call had come to the station, he'd been told the ropy old story about Mary Moore and Fenford Cottage, much as he himself had told the story to Warner. He remembered laughing, and he remembered wondering whether he was being set up for a joke. Eventually, as a young man keen to impress his elders, Lomax had decided to take his bicycle and come out to Fenford Cottage. Not an easy task back in those days, certainly much more difficult than driving, but eventually he'd reached the location. Even now, he could see the old post that he'd used back in the day, when he'd needed to prop his bicycle against something.

Then he'd approached the house.

Nothing seemed to have changed in the intervening year. As he looked out at the building, Lomax remembered opening the gate and making his way toward the front door. He remembered the fear he'd felt in his chest, and the attempts he'd made to calm himself down. He'd knocked on the door several times, and he'd called out, but nobody had answered. The cottage had seemed so utterly empty, so derelict and ignored that there was no way anybody possibly *could* live there. Even as he'd knocked for the third and final time, he'd already come to the conclusion that he'd fallen for a practical joke.

He remembered how cold he'd been that night, almost shivering.

He remembered how he'd stepped back from the house and looked up at the top windows.

He remembered how he'd felt like something of a fool.

On his way back to the bicycle on that cold night, he'd allowed himself a faint smile and he'd told himself to not be so gullible in future. He'd carefully shut the gate, and then he'd climbed back onto his bike. And then, as he'd prepared to cycle back to town, he'd casually glanced back toward the house and he'd seen... *something*… at one of the downstairs windows.

Even now, he felt his conscious mind trying to block the memory.

It was true, though.

Forty years ago, Alan Lomax had spotted what appeared to be a face at one of the windows of Fenford Cottage. He'd spent the rest of his life denying this fact, and for the most part he'd succeeded in convincing himself that the face had been just a trick of the light. Indeed, he recalled that he'd taken a step back toward the gate, and that the face had instantly vanished, which at the time he'd used to further convince himself that he'd been mistaken. And when, over the years, he'd found himself thinking back to that moment, he'd been able to quickly strengthen his belief that the 'face' had only been an illusion.

Each time another new recruit had visited the cottage and come back with nothing to report, this had only gone to prove to Lomax that he'd been wrong. That the face in the window had not been a face at all.

Ever since, however, he'd gone out of his way to avoid driving along this road.

Just in case.

Taking a deep breath, he opened the car door and stepped out. Forty years fell away in a flash and he realized he shouldn't have hidden himself away from Fenford Cottage. He carefully shut the door. Now he realized that he should have confronted his fears head on and shown then to be baseless. He began to walk toward the gate. In a strange way, he felt relieved. He opened the gate and stepped through. Whatever Walker was up to, it would surely prove to be something utterly trivial. He shut the gate, taking care to not make too much noise. How foolish he'd been. Turning, he started walking toward the house, but he forced himself to look not at the window but at the door, until finally he reached the front step and allowed himself a casual glance to the right.

He froze.

The front window, the window where the maybe-a-face had appeared forty years ago, was broken.

"What the..."

Stepping over to take a closer look, he saw that the entire window had been smashed through. The glass had fallen to the inside, so obviously the damage had been caused by somebody trying to break inside. Why, though, would Ben Warner ever do such a thing? For a moment, Lomax could only stare at the shards of glass that still poked out from the frame, and then he made his way closer and peered into the pitch-black cottage.

"Warner?" he hissed. "Are you there?"

Why had he kept his voice low? He had no idea, except that somehow it would have felt wrong to shout. The house was shrouded in darkness, and there was no indication whatsoever that anybody was around. Then again, why would Warner have broken the glass to gain access to the cottage, only to then leave? And if he *had* left, why had he seemingly gone on foot rather than taking the car?

"I say," he continued after a moment, "Warner, are you here? Speak up, man. It's Lomax, I came out here to find out what you're doing."

He waited, but the house offered no response.

"This is utterly absurd," he muttered, although he already knew that turning around and leaving was not an option.

Not again.

Instead, he leaned through the broken window and look around the room, satisfying himself that there was nobody around. There was still a part of him that desperately wanted to just go home, but he'd done that forty years ago and he felt that now he couldn't make the same mistake again. Obviously Warner had gone into the house, and most likely he was still in there. If he still failed to answer, that meant there was a chance that he might have become injured, and Lomax knew full well that he couldn't possibly walk away from such a possibility.

Once he'd brushed some pieces of glass away from the edges of the window, therefore, he began to climb through. At his age, he found the process somewhat difficult, as he struggled to rise his leg high enough. For a moment, he actually began to think that he might be unable to get into the house at all, but finally his pride forced him to push just that little more, and he managed to get his right foot onto the floor inside. He took a moment to get his breath, and then he climbed all the way inside, before reaching out and steadying himself against the wall.

Breathless and a little achy, he took a moment to regather his composure, and then he took a step forward and looked around the room once more.

"Warner!" he called out, daring to raise his voice at least. "Where the hell are you, man?"

AMY CROSS

CHAPTER THIRTEEN

"DID YOU HEAR THAT?" Ben asked, suddenly turning in the darkness to look over his shoulder, back toward the hatch. "I thought I heard a voice."

"Keep your head clear," Mary muttered, scrambling across the wooden beams. "Don't step between the main sections, okay? If you do that, you'll go crashing through."

"How did you get back up here?" he asked, just about able to see her thanks to a patch of moonlight that shone through a hole in the roof.

"There's a second hatch in the bathroom," she explained. "I don't normally use it, because it's smaller and trickier to wriggle through, but it comes in handy occasionally." She turned to him. "What were you doing down there? I told you to get up here!"

"I was coming to help you," he explained.

She rolled her eyes.

"I was!" he insisted. "I'm an officer of the -"

"I know, you're an officer of the law. You've only said it about a million times."

"I was not going to simply crawl up into this space and save my own skin," he continued. "How could you ever expect any man to do such a thing?"

"Maybe I don't have as much faith in people as you do," she replied, before pausing for a moment. "You really, seriously, could have got us both killed just now. I know you think you're in charge, but right now you're way out of your depth. You don't know a single thing about what's happening here, so I think you really ought to listen to me. Do we have an agreement?"

He opened his mouth to tell her that she really should moderate her tone, but then he realized that she might have a point. He genuinely had no idea what was happening, whereas it was apparent that Mary – somehow – knew the situation rather well. In all his twenty-two years, Ben Warner had never really accepted a woman knowing better, yet now he felt that it would be foolish of him to start arguing.

"What's going on here?" he asked finally, with a rather helpless tone to his voice. "Please, from the beginning, just tell me who that woman is, and why she's after you, and who *you* are."

He waited, and for a moment Mary seemed to shocked to know how to respond. She stared at him, and then she looked down at the attic floor as they both heard the creak of footsteps coming from the room beneath.

"It's okay," she continued, "she doesn't ever come up here. She can't, for some reason."

"And who is she?" he asked.

"I..."

Mary's voice trailed off for a few seconds.

"I don't know," she continued finally. "Sometimes I think I should, but I don't. She's a ghost, and -"

"Impossible."

"She's a ghost!"

"Ghosts aren't real."

"You just almost got killed by one!"

He shook his head.

"I get it," she continued, "it's hard to get your head around it, but it's true. All of it. It took me long enough to accept what I was seeing. She's dead, I think she's been dead for a while, but she's still walking around the house, she's still angry."

"I don't believe any of this," Ben replied. "I can't, I'm sorry."

"You will, soon enough."

"What's her name? Have you tried talking to her?"

"She doesn't respond to anything," she

replied. "As for her name, I think she..."

Again, her voice trailed off. She furrowed her brow for a few seconds, almost as if she might be in pain, and then she shook her head.

"And how are *you* caught up in all of this?" he asked. "Let me just get one thing clear right now. You *are* Mary Moore, are you not?"

She nodded.

"Is this your home?" he continued.

"It's really strange," she replied, "but I'm not quite sure what happened. I know my name, but that's about it. I just feel like I've been here forever, I don't remember anything that came before. I think I must have banged my head, because it's as if I just woke up in this house."

"You must come from somewhere."

"I know, but that doesn't help right now!"

"What about Belgravia, in London?"

"Where?"

"It's in the heart of London," he explained. "The reason I came out here tonight is that we received a telephone call from a gentleman who wanted us to check on you. He said that a Miss Mary Moore might be in trouble at Fenford Cottage, and he implored us to come. I didn't get his name, but apparently he's called before." He paused. "How old are you, Mary?"

"I don't know."

"You look twenty, perhaps. Certainly not

thirty."

"I don't know," she said again, with tears in her eyes this time.

"This makes no sense," he continued. "The telephone call was once traced back to an empty house in Belgravia. You must think as hard as you can, Mary. Is there anyone, anyone at all, who might live there who might be concerned about you?"

"I wish I knew."

Sighing, Ben realized that he was rapidly running out of options. The entire case seemed to be unraveling, with none of the parts making sense. All he knew for certain was that, after being chased by some kind of ghastly-looking woman, he was now seemingly trapped in a dark attic with someone who wasn't turning out to be much help. Turning, he looked back toward the hatch as he realized that at some point he was going to have to go back down into the main part of the house.

"Don't," Mary said.

He turned back to her.

"Please," she continued, "don't risk it."

"But if -"

Before he could finish, he heard a faint thudding sound coming from somewhere below in the house. He looked down at the floor, and then he leaned closer to a crack and looked through into the bedroom. There was no sign of the woman, and now the house was silent again. In his entire life, Ben had never felt so utterly helpless; he'd always been able to come up with a plan, even if the situation had seemed dire. Now, for the first time ever, he could see no way to deal with things.

"Tell me the first thing you remember," he said finally, turning to Mary again. "I know you say it's hard, but I need you to try. Tell me the very first thing you remember about being in this house."

CHAPTER FOURTEEN

"THIS IS RIDICULOUS," Inspector Lomax muttered as he stepped out across the darkened front room. "When I find that lad, I'm going to give him a good talking-to and -"

Suddenly hearing a faint bumping sound, he turned and looked over toward the door. The house had already fallen silent again, but he was certain he'd heard... *something*. A footstep, perhaps? No, it had been too light for that. It had been more like somebody brushing against a wall as they walked, and it had seemed close, but now there was no sign of anyone. Somewhere deep down, Lomax felt a flicker of fear, but this was quickly crushed by his absolute sense of duty.

Alan Lomax was not a man who allowed himself to be afraid.

"Listen here, Warner," he said after a moment, still watching the doorway, "I won't have any silly business, do you understand? If you're here, then you'd bloody well better come out into the open and explain yourself. Is that clear?"

He waited, and there was no reply, but he felt absolutely certain that Warner could hear him. Although he was not accustomed to vagaries and superstitions, he couldn't shake the strong sense that somebody was nearby. Even as he reached back and scratched the back of his neck, it was as if he could feel a presence getting closer and closer in the room. He just couldn't *see* that presence.

"I suppose it's true what they say," he added finally. "If you want a job done properly, do it yourself."

He took a step forward, before suddenly spinning around as he felt something touch his left shoulder. It was as if a hand had momentarily materialized out of nowhere, yet now there was quite clearly nobody behind him. He looked around again, feeling rather uncomfortable, but then he managed to remind himself that everything appeared completely normal. Taking a deep breath, he turned and made his way out into the hallway.

Stopping at the bottom of the stairs, he listened for a moment, but there was no sign of anybody. He almost made his way up to the top floor, but then he decided instead to check the kitchen first.

Walking through to the back of the house, he stopped in the kitchen and once again looked around. The place appeared to be completely deserted, and the broken window remained the only hint that Warner had forced an entry. Lomax had always been a straightforward man, and he expected other people to be straightforward in return, so he felt increasingly irritated by the fact that he was being left in the dark. Finally, supposing that he'd have to try upstairs, he turned to go back through to the hallway.

In a flash, he spotted something moving next to his left shoulder. He stepped back in shock, but there was nothing now, and he quickly told himself that the 'something' must have been his own shadow. He held his hand out, trying to recreate the effect but with no luck. He swallowed hard, once again having to ignore the tiniest inkling of fear in his belly, and then he headed back through to the hallway. One way or another, he was going to sort matters out.

And then, stopping at the bottom of the stairs, he once again hesitated as he spotted a door a little way further along, seemingly leading under the staircase itself. He briefly considered going up to the first floor, but then he headed over to the door and pulled it open. Leaning into the darkness, he immediately felt cold air against his face, so he took the torch from his belt and switched it on, before shining the light down into the darkness. Just as he'd suspected, he saw a set of stone steps heading into what could only be the house's basement.

"Warner!" he hissed. "Are you down there?"

He waited, but there was no reply. He supposed he should check upstairs first, but at the same time he told himself that he might as well look in the basement first, just in case he stumbled upon Warner. After all, the lad seemed to be consciously hiding, in which case Lomax was determined to get to the bottom of things once and for all, so he pushed the door all the way open and then he began to pick his way carefully down to the space beneath the house.

Immediately, he felt cobwebs against his face, so he brushed them aside as he made his way down to the bottom of the steps. By now, he was starting to think that he should have gone to the house's top floor first, but instead of turning back he walked out into the middle of the basement and shone the torch's beam around. All he saw at first were empty shelves that had been pushed against the walls, although after a moment he spotted some boxes in the far corner. He headed over and looked down into one of the boxes, and to his surprise he saw what appeared to be dolls.

Lots of dolls.

Reaching into the box, he picked up a

floppy rag doll, obviously something once owned by a child. The doll was faded and tattered, as if it had once seen a lot of use, and Lomax couldn't help but smile. Setting the doll back down, he picked up another, and then another, and then he found that there were also some clothes in the box. These, too, had clearly once belonged to a child. Everything had been very neatly folded before being placed in the box, and a moment later he spotted some books as well.

Picking up the first book, he saw that it was a collection of verses for children. He opened to the first page, and to his surprise he saw an inscription written in faint, barely-legible pencil. Squinting, he was finally able to make out the words:

This books belongs to
Mary Moore

There was that name, the same name from the telephone calls. In all his time in Bilside, Lomax had never uncovered any evidence whatsoever to suggest that Mary Moore was even a real person, but now it was clear that she was. Or, at least, that she had been once, since everything in the box seemed to be very faded.

Realizing that he was allowing himself to get sidetracked, Lomax carefully set the book back down. There would be time to delve further into the mystery of Fenford Cottage, but for now he was more concerned with the task of tracking down his wayward sergeant.

Turning, he began to head back over to the stairs, when suddenly he froze as he saw a human figure standing in the far corner, barely visible in the darkness. Stunned by this development, Lomax merely stared for a moment, not daring to say a word, not even daring to aim his torch's beam in that direction. Instead, he hesitated for a little longer, before taking a step toward the figure.

"Who's there?" he asked cautiously. "I say, I'm a police officer, and I demand to know who you are."

He could see now, from the shape of the silhouette that this was a lady, although she seemed remarkably tall. He raised his torch a little, hoping to get a better view without – of course – shining the beam directly into her eyes. As he raised the torch further, however, he got a better view of the figure's bare feet, and he realized that the feet seemed to be somehow hovering in mid-air, a good twenty or thirty inches above the concrete floor.

"What the blazes?" Lomax muttered, as he raised the torch further, finally illuminating the full figure.

In that instant, his heart seemed to freeze as he saw the full horror of what was before him. He stepped closer, barely able to believe the truth, but as he slowly raised the torch's beam he finally understood the true nature of the awful figure. He stared, numb to his core, and then – realizing that he absolutely had to run and fetch help – he turned to leave.

And that was when he saw the ghostly figure standing right behind him. Before he had time to react, she stepped closer and screamed.

CHAPTER FIFTEEN

Some time earlier...

FLAT ON HER BACK, she opened her eyes and blinked a few times in the bright morning light, and then she tried to answer the simple question that was burning in her mind.

Where am I?

As she began to sit up, she felt more than a little sore and achy. She soon found that she was on the floor in what appeared to be a fair ordinary and conventional front room, although she was too groggy to quite get her thoughts straight. She rubbed her eyes and then she tucked her hair back behind her ears, but still she was unable to work out exactly where she was or how she'd ended up there. All she really knew for certain was that the place felt familiar.

Getting to her feet, she headed over to the window and peered outside. She immediately felt reassured by the sight of the front garden, and by the path that wound its way to the gate. Beyond that, there was the main road, which she somehow instinctively knew ran from the town. Bilton? Bilford? It took a moment before she remembered the proper name.

"Bilside," she whispered.

Suddenly hearing a bumping sound, she turned and looked over her shoulder. Was there somebody else in the house? That was a possibility that she hadn't considered until now, so she stood completely still and listened. Who else *could* be in the house, anyway? That was another question, and she felt as if all the answers were hidden behind a kind of foggy cloud in the back of her mind. She could remember sensations, and feelings, but not actual facts.

Except her name.

She remembered her name.

Mary Moore. Of that, at least, she was certain. Her name seemed to be burning in her mind, almost as if some deep part of her consciousness was frantically keen to make sure that it couldn't follow all the other facts into a void. The problem, however, was that for the moment her name seemed to exist in isolation, cut off from any other knowledge about her life, and there was no sign that the fog in her mind was about to lift.

A moment later, hearing another bump, she turned and looked once more at the doorway that led through to the hall.

"Who's there?" she called out, and then she held her breath as she waited for a reply.

After a few seconds, she forced herself to go over to the door. The entire house seemed eerily silent now, but the silence seemed to be anticipating something that was about to happen. Even as she stopped in the doorway, Mary felt as if she was about to hear another bump at any moment, yet at the same time she was also sure about one other thing: she had been in the house before, and she had been alone.

"Come on," she whispered, hoping to jog her memories a little, "try to remember."

Reaching up, she began to touch the sides of her head, searching for any evidence of an injury. That was what usually caused people to forget things, right? Finding nothing, however, she began to worry that something more serious must be wrong. It was as if all the memories were in her head somewhere, but they slipped just out of reach every time she tried to find them.

Suddenly a loud, piercing scream rang out.

Stepping back, Mary listened in horror as the scream faded. It had seemed to come from everywhere at once, although after a moment she looked over toward the door that led down into the basement. Somehow, she had a very clear image of the steps beyond the door, but she hesitated as she tried to remember when and how she'd been down there before. In her mind's eye, she could remember slowly making her way down with only a candle to light her way, and even now she felt a cold, hard dread starting to press against her chest.

She took another step back, and now she realized she could hear somebody sobbing somewhere in the house. The sound filled her with a sense of dread, because she immediately knew that she'd heard the voice somewhere before. Whoever was sobbing, they were someone familiar, and Mary felt a growing sense of panic at the realization that she still couldn't remember anything about her life. She knew she should probably rush to help the other person, but a growing sense of fear caused her to linger near the doorway, and finally – in a sudden rush of panic – she slammed the door shut.

Now at least she could no longer hear the sobbing, but she kept her eyes fixed on the door as she moved back to the middle of the room. Her mind might have been refusing to surrender its memories, but her body seemed to know that the other person in the house was to be avoided at all costs.

A moment later, hearing a bumping sound

coming from the hallway, Mary instinctively turned and ran behind one of the armchairs, and then she crouched down to hide. She was trembling now, terrified of something she couldn't even remember, and then her fear intensified as she heard the sound of the door very slowly creaking open.

She held her breath.

Please, don't find me.

For a few seconds, there was only silence, and she allowed herself to hope that she'd not be discovered. Too scared to even try looking around the side of the chair, she stared down at the floor and waited. And then, finally, she heard a very slow but very deliberate footstep, followed by another, then another.

Coming closer.

Coming toward the armchair.

Please please please please please. Just leave me alone.

She tried to curl into the smallest shape possible, even though she knew that all hope was lost. The footsteps stopped, and then very slowly the chair began to move aside. Mary turned away, terrified of what she might see if she looked up, until finally the chair was all the way out. Still trembling, Mary squeezed her eyes tight shut and waited for whatever might happen next, but she knew that she was being watched.

Please don't hurt me. Please.

After a few minutes, however, she began to wonder why she hadn't yet been attacked. The fear was still strong in her chest, but she forced herself to open her eyes. Staring down at the floor, she tried to muster the courage to look up, but at first she found herself frozen by fear. Finally, somehow, she found the strength to turn and see the figure that was towering above her.

I know you.

I just don't remember how.

Staring up at the dead face, Mary instantly recognized the woman.

CHAPTER SIXTEEN

Some time later...

"AND THAT'S IT?" Ben asked, after Mary had fallen silent at the end of telling her story. "You don't remember anything at all from before you woke up in the house?"

She shook her head. On her knees in the attic, with a patch of moonlight falling through the gap in the ceiling and catching the side of her face, she looked utterly lost for words.

"Ever since that moment," she said, her voice trembling with fear, "I've been trapped here. I've tried to leave, but it's impossible. Sometimes she leaves me alone for a while, other times she comes at me with such fury. It's as if she hates me, but I don't even know who she is, I swear!"

Ben thought for a moment.

"Is it possible," he said finally, "that she's your mother?"

"How could that monster possibly be my mother?" Mary asked.

"The age difference would seem to be about right," he pointed out. "Perhaps you lived here with her, and for some reason you no longer remember any of that."

"And now my dead mother's haunting me?"

"She's not dead," he replied firmly. "She can't be. Ghosts just..."

His voice trailed off for a moment, as he began to realize that the entire situation felt impossible. He wanted easy answers, and he was rapidly coming to understand that there would be none.

"Let's assume that you're right," he said with a sigh. "I'm not saying that you are, but just for a moment... Why would any ghost be so determined to torment you? Obviously she either can't or won't harm you in any way, so why is she doing all this?"

"I don't know," Mary replied desperately.

"How long ago did you wake up here?"

"It feels like forever."

"It can't be forever. Are we talking a day? A week?"

"Longer, I think."

"But that's not possible," he continued. "At

the station, Inspector Lomax said that the phone call has been going on for years, but you're not old enough for that to be true."

"I don't know what to tell you," she replied.

"I need you to try harder," he explained. "Really think back to -"

"I don't know!" she screamed, suddenly getting to her feet. "Why can't you understand that? I don't know, and you can't change that by telling me to try! Don't you think I've been doing that ever since I woke up here?"

"Mary -"

"You have no idea what it's like to not know who you are or where you came from!" she yelled, before putting her hands on her face and starting to sob wildly. "I'm trapped, going round and round, being chased from room to room. Every time I think I've come up with a way to leave, I go down there and it never works. I end up back here in the attic. It's hopeless!"

"No situation is ever hopeless," Ben told her. "You have my word, we're going to get out of here. Both of us."

"She won't let us leave," Mary said again. "Can you try to get that into your head? Once you've seen her, that's it, you're trapped here forever. I don't know all the rules of how this thing works, but that's one of them. Believe me, I've tried. If it was at all possible to escape, I'd be out of here by now."

"So what are you suggesting?" he asked. "Are you saying that we should simply stay up here indefinitely?"

"There's no way out of the house," she sobbed.

"I absolutely refuse to accept that," he replied, before getting to his feet and carefully making his way over to the hole in the roof. Barely the size of a single tile, the hole wasn't even large enough for a man to get his hand through, let alone his entire body.

"I already tried that," she told him, as he tried in vain to make the hole larger. "It's just not going to happen."

He tried for a moment longer, before accepting that this particular approach wasn't going to work. Taking a step back, he thought for a moment, and then he looked over at Mary again.

"You can't have tried everything," he said firmly. "One way or another, I assure you, we are getting out of this house. Right now."

Stepping over to the hatch, he hesitated before starting to open it carefully.

"Don't!" Mary whispered.

"I don't think she's down there right now," he replied, keeping his voice low. Once the hatch was fully open, he leaned down to check. "The bedroom's empty."

"She could appear at any moment!"

"Is that what happens?" he asked, turning back to her. "Because I was in the house for quite some time before I saw her. Perhaps she's not always here."

"You just have to accept that we're trapped here."

"How can you do that?" he replied, before looking down once again into the bedroom. "She's not there," he continued, "and even if she *does* appear, I'll be better prepared this time. I highly doubt that a frail old woman can cause me much harm, especially when she no longer has the benefit of surprising me. And if you're right and she turns out to be a ghost then, well, I have even less to fear. Now, come on, let's get moving."

With that, he lowered himself back down into the room, landing carefully and quietly on the bed. His attempt to reason with Mary had left him feeling a little more confident, although he still dreaded the awful sight of the woman coming closer. So far, so good, however, and as he stepped down off the bed he told himself that he could handle anything that was thrown at him. After all, he was an officer of the law, and he believed that his training would prove invaluable.

After a moment, he looked back up at the hatch and saw Mary's terrified face staring down at him.

"Well?" he said. "Are you coming?"

"I... I can't," she stammered. "Please, come back up."

"Then I shall come back for you shortly," he said firmly. "With back-up."

"She won't let you go!" Mary hisses, as he turned and started walking to the door. "Don't do this! Come back!"

Reaching the doorway, Ben looked around, and there was still no sign of the woman. It was as if she had vanished into thin air, and he noted that perhaps this was what had happened. He still couldn't quite bring himself to believe that there was a ghost in the house, but he quickly told himself that he could deal with anything that he came across. Indeed, as he stepped out onto the landing and made his way to the top of the stairs, he felt supremely confident that he was about to get to the bottom of all the mysteries of Fenford Cottage.

"Please!" Mary hissed, as he began to walk downstairs. "Come back!"

CHAPTER SEVENTEEN

THE STEP AT THE bottom of the stairs creaked loudly as Ben reached the hallway. He shone the beam from his torch all around, to check that there was no sign of the woman, and then he made his way to the front room. With each step, he expected to suddenly spot movement nearby, but finally he got to the broken window, and he stopped to look out at the dark garden.

He could see the front of his patrol car, just poking out from behind the bushes that lined the road.

So close, yet so far.

At least he had a plan now. He was going to get to the car and drive into town, and he was going to wake Inspector Lomax up and tell him everything that had happened. He knew he probably wouldn't be believed, at least not at first, but he was determined to make sure that several officers accompanied him back out to the house. Then they could really get to the bottom of what was happening. Then, finally, they'd discover the truth about Mary Moore.

He glanced around one more time, to make doubly sure that there was still no sign of the woman, and then he began to climb out through the window.

Suddenly something grabbed him from behind, digging sharp fingers into his shoulders. He heard a loud snarling sound as he was pulled back and sent crashing to the floor, and then he looked up just in time to see the ghostly woman fade from view. For a moment, too shocked to comprehend what had just happened, Ben could only stare in horror at the space where she'd been standing.

His heart was racing, but he knew what he had to do.

He had to try again. And this time, he'd be more prepared.

Getting to his feet, he told himself that he'd have to force his way out of the house. Perhaps the woman would appear again, but in that case he was willing to restrain her if necessary. Still, he couldn't help but stare at the spot where he'd last seen her, and he was struggling to come up with an explanation as to how she'd simply disappeared. He still wasn't quite able to accept that the woman could be a ghost, even if his defenses were crumbling and he was beginning to run out of alternative ideas.

He took a step forward, braced for the figure to appear again at any moment.

"I'm an officer of the law," he said under his breath, hoping to steady his own nerves a little. "I'm an officer of the law. I'm an officer of the -"

Suddenly he stopped as he reached the window. He'd been planning to climb straight out, but now he found that he was gripped instead by an overwhelming sense of dread. Staring down at the few pieces of broken glass that were still poking out from the frame, he looked at the jagged edges and imagined them cutting deep into his flesh. At first, that thought horrified him, but then a growing sense of anticipation began to creep its way up through his body, until finally he reached out and began to pull one of the shards loose. This took a moment, but soon he was able to place the glass against his wrist.

Why fight?

Why try to get back to the rest of the world, when the rest of the world was so lonely and dull? Since arriving in Bilside, he'd been renting a room in a house on the edge of town, and he'd found his landlady to be rather tough and abrasive. Each night, he retired to his room and sat alone, trying to amuse himself by reading, but in truth he felt dreadfully out of place. He'd been telling himself over and over that things would eventually get better, yet now he began to realize that there was no point waiting. Why struggle to get back to that life, when he could just end all the misery right now?

He slowly began to drag the glass across his wrist. The skin stretched, but there wasn't enough pressure to cause an actual cut.

He prepared to try again.

As soon as he took a step forward, however, the sense of dread returned. He thought again of the room, although this time his anger felt different. He'd been betrayed, left to rot, forgotten by the world. Someone had abandoned him, had dropped him to the side and failed to care. He had no idea who this person could be, but the thoughts were drifting deeper and deeper into his mind until he almost seemed to be experiencing feelings and memories from another life. The anger, in particular, seemed so strange and unusual, yet it was consuming him until he felt as if he was about to scream. Finally, he began to squeeze the glass tight in his right hand. Somehow, the pain seemed to help.

"I'll make you pay," he sneered. "I'll make you regret the day you walked out of this house."

As the pain became stronger and stronger in his hand, he imagined somebody suffering. There was a specific person who had to feel pain, but he had no idea who that person was; he was filled with hate, but the hate seemed to be flowing in from somewhere else. All he knew was that the world had become a dark and cruel place, and that eventually everyone would see that they'd done the wrong thing. He wanted them all to know the truth, but that would mean making the ultimate sacrifice. Squeezing even harder on the piece of glass, he began to smile as he imagined the moment when it would all come out.

"What am I doing?" he stammered, suddenly dropping the piece of glass and taking a step back.

For a moment, he simply stood and tried to work out what had happened. A moment later he looked at his right hand and saw blood dribbling down the sides. Opening his fingers, he was shocked to find that he'd managed to dig the glass deep into his palm. He'd been consumed by a sense of pure hatred, but somehow it had been somebody else's hatred. He had no idea how that had worked, but never in all his life had he ever experienced such a sensation. Now, as he stood alone in the front room, he was beginning to feel more like his old self, and he realized that he'd inadvertently taken a step back from the window.

He stepped forward, and the anger immediately began to return. Startled, he stepped back again, and the anger faded as he realized that he didn't dare try again. Something about going to the window seemed to fill him with the most terrible ideas.

"That's one of the ways she does it."

Turning, he saw Mary standing in the doorway. She glanced over her shoulder, as if she was worried that the woman might appear again, and then she turned back to him.

"Do you get it now?" she continued. "It's like she projects these feelings into you any time you try to escape. If you don't believe me, go on, try again."

He hesitated, before looking over at the window again. He knew that he had to find a way out of the cottage, but at the same time there was absolutely no way he could allow himself to feel so much anger and misery. By the time he looked back over at Mary, he was starting to feel genuinely lost.

"You're trapped here now," she said, "like me. It never ends. Sometimes I wish she'd just kill me and get it over with, but it's almost as if she likes toying with me. Maybe it'll be different now that you're here, but I'm not so sure. I'm sorry you didn't get out in time. I should have found a way to warn you sooner, but I was just too scared."

Lost for words, he looked again at the window, but he still couldn't muster the courage to go any closer. He felt as if all the possibilities had been exhausted, as if there was nothing left to try, yet still his mind was whirring as he tried to come up with some new plan. He'd never really experienced true hopelessness before, not until arriving at Fenford Cottage, and the sensation was... unpleasant, to say the least.

"There has to be something we can do," he said finally, heading over to the doorway and squeezing past Mary. "Where is she? Maybe I can talk to her."

"That won't work."

"I have to try."

"I told you it -"

"Hello!" he called out, cupping his hands around his mouth as he looks up the stairs. "Wherever you are, can you show yourself? I don't know exactly what's happening, but I'm sure we can come to an agreement! I can help you, but first I need to know what you want!"

He waited, but there was no answer. It was almost as if the woman had left the house entirely. Exasperated, he looked around, and that was when he once again noticed the door leading to a space under the stairs.

"What's in there?" he muttered, before stepping over to take a look.

"No!" Mary shouted, suddenly stepping in front of him to block his way, her face filled with terror. "You can't go down there!"

CHAPTER EIGHTEEN

"WHYEVER NOT?" Ben asked, shocked by the vehemence of Mary's sudden warning.

"You just can't!" she said firmly, stepping back and holding her hands out in another attempt to hold him back. "There's nothing down there!"

"I'd like to see that for myself," he said cautiously.

She shook her head.

"Have you been down there?" he asked.

"It's just the basement," she explained. "That's all. It's just a big, empty basement."

"If it's empty, then -"

"Just listen to me!" she yelled frantically. "I've already checked it out, and there's nothing there, okay? There's no time to go rummaging about and wasting time, we have to get back up to the attic!"

Ben hesitated for a moment, before taking a step toward her. He expected to be overcome by a wave of dread and anger, just as had happened at the window, but he felt no change. Mary's sudden outburst seemed to be unconnected to any attempt to keep the pair of them in the house, in which case he couldn't help but wonder why she was so absolutely keen for him to stay out of the basement. One thing was for sure: he knew now that he had to go down there and take a look for himself.

"Please step out of the way," he said.

"No."

"What is it that you don't want me to see?"

"There's nothing!" she snarled through clenched teeth. "Why won't you listen to me?"

Reaching out, he tried to push her aside, but she resisted. Reluctant to use too much force, he hesitated as he tried to understand the sheer terror in her eyes. Already, he could tell that something horrific must have happened to Mary when she went down into the basement before, and he knew that he had to get to the truth.

"Please," he said softly, hoping that a more conciliatory tone might help, "even if you wait up here, I have to see. There has to be an answer to this misery somewhere, and I've been everywhere else in the house. If there's even a chance of finding a solution down there in the basement, you can't stop me going down."

With tears in her eyes, she shook her head.

"What is it?" he asked. "Tell me."

"I don't know," she stammered. "Honestly, I don't. I don't remember. All I know is that I went down there and... that's when I first saw her. I think so, anyway. My mind is so foggy, but I think I went down into the basement, and maybe that's when I woke her up. She wasn't angry before then."

Ben opened his mouth to ask another question, but then he held back. Until that moment, he'd managed to keep himself from accepting that something supernatural might be happening in the house, he'd been able somehow to come up with twisted arguments that almost explained what he'd seen, but now he could feel his defenses crumbling. There was no possible rational explanation for the woman he'd seen, other than that she must have been a ghost. And if that indeed turned out to be the case, then all bets were off.

Suddenly he realized he could hear a faint scratching sound.

"Where's that coming from?" he asked.

"What?" Mary replied, before turning and looking down at the bottom of the door.

"Is that her?" Ben continued, sure now that something was scratching at the door's other side, right down by the floor.

"I've never heard that before," Mary said,

taking a step back.

"Does this house have rats?" Ben asked. "Mice?"

"Nothing of that nature," she replied.

He paused, before reaching for the handle.

Mary immediately grabbed his wrist.

"We have to see," Ben said firmly. "You say you think you woke the woman up by going down to the basement. Have you been down there since?"

"Of course not."

"Then maybe that's what we have to do."

He waited for her to put up another argument, but a moment later her hand slipped away from his wrist. She was still clearly terrified but, as she took another step back, it seemed that she was willing to let him take the lead.

Turning back to the door, he felt a pang of fear in his chest, yet at the same time he knew what he had to do. He took hold of the handle, and then he turned it slowly as the scratching sound continued, and then finally he began to pull the basement door open.

"Help me!" Inspector Lomax gasped.

"Sir!"

Reaching down, Ben immediately grabbed the older man's arms and began to pull him all the way up the steps. Lomax was shivering wildly, as if convulsed by some terrible fear that had taken him over entirely, but he gripped Ben's arms in a desperate attempt to reach safety. His legs, seemingly useless now, dragged up from the top step, and finally Ben lay Lomax down as Mary hurriedly pushed the door shut.

"Sir, what are you doing here?" Ben asked, filled with panic as he looked for any sign of injury. "What happened?"

Lomax tried to say something, but he could get no words out. The man's entire body seemed to be shuddering violently, and his eyes were filled with a stare of absolute horror, almost as if he was still seeing whatever had caused him to fall into such an awful state. Again, he grabbed Ben's arm, as if for reassurance, and he seemed to be trying to say something even as a choking sound began to rattle in the back of his throat.

"I have to get him out of here," Ben said, turning to Mary. "This must be some kind of cardiac arrest."

"You can't," she replied.

"He's dying!" Ben hissed, before looking back down at Lomax. "Sir, if you can hear me, everything's going to be alright."

"The most we can do is try to get him to the attic," Mary suggested.

"We are not cowering in that attic!" Ben snapped. "You're going to help me carry him out of here, right now, and that's an order!"

"But the window!"

"We'll find another way!"

"Not the front door," she replied, holding her hands up to show her stubbed, bloodied fingertips. "Do you seriously think I haven't tried every possible means of escape?"

"Then -"

Before he could finish, Ben heard Lomax let out an anguished gasp. Looking down, he realized that Lomax was looking at Mary, and that the sight of her seemed to have sent him into paroxysms of fear. Desperately trying to pull away from her, Lomax began trying to shout something at Mary, even as he clung more firmly than ever to Ben's arm.

"It's okay," Ben told him, "she's just -"

"Keep her away from me!" Lomax screamed, finally managing to get the words out. "Don't let her touch me!"

"What does he mean?" Mary asked, looking at Ben. "Why's he saying that? I've never seen this man before in my life!"

"You have to stop her!" Lomax yelled, suddenly kicking out hard at Mary, forcing her to pull away. "Don't give her what she wants!"

CHAPTER NINETEEN

"SIR, PLEASE," BEN SAID, as Lomax crawled toward the front door, "what happened to you in the basement?"

Muttering something incomprehensible, Lomax reached up toward the handle, but he was unable to raise his body far enough off the floor. He let out a series of pained gasps as he tried again and again, before finally slumping back down. Slowly, he rolled onto his side and looked back at Ben, and then he stared directly toward Mary.

"I don't know who you are," she sobbed, with tears running down her face, "and I promise, I've never hurt you! I never would! I could never do anything bad to another human being!"

"There must have been some kind of mistake," Ben suggested. "Sir, this is Mary Moore, the woman who was always mentioned in those phone calls. I can't even begin to explain what's happening here, but the situation is..."

He paused, trying to think of the right word.

"Strange," he added finally. "And dire."

"I've never hurt anyone in my life," Mary said, turning to him. "Please, you have to believe me."

"Get away!" Lomax screamed. "Sergeant Warner, don't let that woman anywhere near you! That's an order!"

"Why's he saying these things?" Mary asked. "I don't understand!"

"Sir, I can assure you that Mary is a good person," Ben said, stepping over to where Lomax was once again trying to reach the handle. "Can you please tell me what happened to you down in that basement? I was about to go down myself, is there... I know this might sound like a foolish question, but is there someone down there?"

"Mary Moore is a monster," Lomax replied, straining yet again to grab the handle, as his face reddened with the effort. "Don't let her near you, Warner. We should never have disturbed her. Don't give her what she wants. Do you understand? She's pure evil, she..."

He hesitated, before letting out a faint gasp. Then, slowly, he slithered back down to the floor, before rolling onto his back.

"Sir?"

Ben waited, but Lomax's eyes were wide open and after a moment it became apparent that he was no longer breathing.

"Sir!"

Immediately remembering his training, Ben straddled the older man and began to administer aid. He tried everything he could think of, but Lomax's lifeless body failed to respond. For several minutes, Ben worked as hard as he could, even as he began to realize that matters were hopeless. He persevered long after he knew that the situation was hopeless, and finally he only stopped as he realized that his chest compressions had begun to break Lomax's ribs. Sitting back, he stared down at the corpse and saw a pair of dead eyes staring up toward the ceiling.

He'd failed.

It had been his job to save Inspector Lomax, and now the man was gone.

After a moment, he turned and looked over at Mary. She was cowering in the corner, staring at the scene in horror, but she seemed too terrified to move or to say anything. All around them, the house was now completely silent.

"He's dead," Ben said finally. "I've never... I've never seen a dead body before."

Climbing off Lomax, he crawled over to the wall and leaned back. He felt weak, as if he might pass out at any moment.

"That's crazy for a police officer to say, isn't it?" he continued, looking down at his trembling hands. "I just never saw one while I was training, and tonight was my first night on the job in Bilside, so..."

His voice trailed off. He couldn't help replaying Lomax's final moments over and over again, trying to work out whether there was anything he could have done differently. A few seconds later, hearing a shuffling sound, he turned and saw that Mary was crawling toward him. She stopped, however, as their eyes met.

"Mary Moore is a monster," Ben heard Lomax's voice saying, echoing in his memory. "Don't let her near you, Warner. We should never have disturbed her. Don't give her what she wants. Do you understand? She's pure evil, she..."

Those had been his final words. Inspector Alan Lomax had been one of the most admirable men Ben had ever met, and now he found it impossible to ignore words that even now repeated over and over in his thoughts. The more he stared at Mary, the more he began to realize that there was so much about her that didn't make sense, and that he had absolutely no reason to believe her claims. Certainly, if it came down to a choice between Lomax and Mary, it was the former who had to be trusted.

"I don't know why he said those things," Mary stammered finally, as if she'd read his mind. "Please, you have to believe me, I've never hurt anyone in my life, and I never saw that man before he come up from the basement just now. You *do* believe me, don't you?"

He opened his mouth to reassure her, but no words emerged. The more he looked at Mary, the more he felt himself starting to distrust her.

"I'm begging you," she continued, "don't believe those things he said. I don't know what he meant, but I swear he had no reason to be scared of me." She paused. "Please," she added after a few seconds, "tell me you believe me."

"I don't know what I believe," he replied cautiously. "The one thing I know, however, is that there's something very wrong in this house. And, frankly, hiding from the truth hasn't helped anyone, so it's time to get to the bottom of it."

"That's what we've been trying to do, isn't it?" she said, before forcing a smile. "Hey, let's get back up to the attic before the woman appears again. It's been a while since we last saw her, she'll be here soon."

Still staring at her, Ben felt his suspicions beginning to grow.

"Let's go," she continued, getting to her feet and reaching a hand out toward him. "Please. Now. Let's go back to the attic."

"There's nothing in the attic," he pointed out.

"But we're safe there! She can't get us while we're in the attic!"

"We'll rot in the attic."

"But we'll be safe."

As Ben stood, Mary hurried over to him and grabbed his hand, and then she tried to pull him toward the stairs.

"We have to hurry!" she insisted, sounding more and more desperate. "Please, don't risk letting her find us again! The only safe thing to do is go to the attic, and then we can try to come up with another plan. You understand that, don't you? We have to go to the attic!"

She pulled on his hand, harder this time.

"The attic!" she hissed.

"No," he replied, pulling his hand free.

"Yes!" She tried to grab his hand again, but this time he pushed her away. "We can't wait!"

"A man is dead," Ben replied, glancing down at Lomax's body for a moment before turning back to her, "and I am a police officer. I can't hide away and hope that things get better. I can't profess to have any clue as to what's really happening in this house tonight, but I know that I have a duty to perform. Part of that duty means getting to the bottom of this whole situation, and it seems to me right now that there's only one way to do that."

He paused, before turning and looking over at the door that led down to the basement.

"No," Mary whimpered softly, "please, no..."

Ignoring her, he stepped over to the door. His heart was racing, for he knew that something in the basement had killed Inspector Lomax, but he felt absolutely certain that he had to go down and see for himself. As he reached for the handle, he knew that part of himself wanted to turn and run, but he managed to force himself to stay strong.

"You can't go down there," Mary sobbed. "Please, you don't understand."

Pulling the door open, Ben saw the concrete stairs leading deep down into the cold, pitch-black space beneath the house. He took his torch from his belt and switched it on, and then he took a deep breath before starting to make his way down into the darkness.

"No!" Mary screamed suddenly, her voice piercing the silence of the house. "Don't do it!"

CHAPTER TWENTY

THE AIR WAS ICY as he reached the bottom of the stairs. Shining his torch ahead, Ben saw a large, empty space with some shelves set against the far wall. So far, there was no sign of movement at all, but at the same time he felt he could sense a presence. He told himself that this was impossible, yet the feeling persisted and – if anything – began to get stronger.

"Please!" Mary called out from the top of the stairs, not daring to follow him down. "You have to get out of there! Now!"

Paying not attention to her words, Ben began to make his way forward. His footsteps seemed too loud, and he worried that he was disturbing some great silence that had lain undisturbed for so long at the bottom of the house.

After a moment he spotted something familiar on the floor, and he crouched down to take a look.

Lomax's torch, albeit with the glass broken and the bulb destroyed.

Getting to his feet, Ben headed over to the shelves, but they were almost entirely bare. A few old tins of food had been left behind, and after a moment Ben realized that there were yet more unanswered questions in the house. How was Mary managing to survive, given that she seemingly had no access to food or water? Two, three days at most would be the maximum someone could be expected to last, so he supposed that Mary could not have been in the house for any longer than that.

He turned and shone the torch around. At first he saw nothing untoward, but then he noticed that there was another section of the basement, running off from an arch in the corner. He'd almost missed this section, since it was almost hidden behind some more shelves. Now he wandered over and shone the torch's beam along what turned out to be a short corridor that led to another room. He glanced over his shoulder, to check that he was still alone, and then he began to walk along the corridor.

Somehow, the air seemed to be getting even colder.

Stopping in another doorway, he shone the torch through, and in an instant he spotted a human shape on the floor. Even before he began to make his way over, he somehow knew that this shape was a human body, and a moment later he spotted an overturned chair and a rope hanging from the ceiling. He stepped closer, aiming the torch's beam down, and finally he saw the truth: a dead woman lay on the floor, her bones poking out from within a faded and tattered black dress. Some patches of skin still clung to her skull, along with thin white hair, but her eyes were gone and it was evident that she had been dead for many years. Decades, even.

He crouched down to take a closer look, but already he couldn't help noticing that the dress seemed familiar. It was, indeed, the same as the dress worn by the ghostly woman.

Looking up, he saw a rope dangling from the ceiling. When he peered down at the corpse, he saw another section of rope tied around the neck, and now he had no doubts as to what had happened. The woman had hung herself, and her body had remained undiscovered ever since.

A moment later, he saw a piece of paper on the floor. Reaching over, he pulled it closer and saw that it was covered in handwriting, and that it seemed to be some kind of letter. He struggled at first to read any of the words, but finally he was able to decipher the message:

December 6th, 1872

To whomsoever discovers me in this state, I ask only that I am given a burial. I know that I cannot be put to rest in consecrated ground, not after what I have done, but a simple grave will suffice. I ask for no headstone.

Let it be known that I die this way because of the actions of others. I always believed in the power and purity of love, but in the end it was love that killed me. I trusted a man who betrayed me, and who tempted me until I became a spent and sin-filled fool. There is no going back from that. I was tested, and I failed.

His name is Malcolm Renshaw and he lives at number nine, Fitzharlow Street, in Belgravia, London. I shall not detail his crimes against me here, for the list would seem petty, but I should like to warn all people to stay away from him. He is not fit to entertain, nor to spend time in the company of ladies. I was a lady when I first met him, even if he lured me down a path of deviation.

I expect no mercy, and little pity. I end my life because I know that there is no chance of restoration, my soul's damnation is complete. I was not always this weak, but in my fifty-seventh years I have fallen too far to ever recover. I pray that the Lord shall judge me fairly, I know that he will.

Mary Elizabeth Moore
Fenford Cottage

Mary Moore? He read that name over and over, convinced that it had to be a mistake, but then he lowered the letter as he realized that there had to be some other explanation. Perhaps, he supposed finally, the young Mary was the older Mary's namesake, but that raised fresh questions as well. Why would the young Mary not remember her place in the family? And how did she end up abandoned and neglected in the house?

He read the letter for a second time, determined to make sure that he had missed nothing. No fresh truths were revealed, however, and finally he looked back over at the poor dead woman.

"It was you," he whispered as he thought back to how he'd felt earlier at the window. "How did you do that?"

The idea seemed absurd, but at the same time he was certain that he'd somehow experienced the same feelings and the same anger that he now read about in the letter. It was as if, for a moment, he'd been filled with the despair that this woman had felt when she killed herself. He knew this was impossible, of course, yet the idea lingered in his mind until finally he set the letter down. The emotions had been so strong at the window, and he was terrified of feeling them again. Getting to his feet, he looked down at the dead woman, and then suddenly he sensed something moving nearby.

Looking ahead, he saw the ghostly figure watching him.

He froze, too terrified to move, as he stared at her dead eyes. Whereas before she'd been screaming, now she seemed content to simply observe him, although he felt certain that she'd attack at any moment. After a few seconds he managed to take a step back, and then he hesitated in case she became angry. He was shivering now in the icy air of the basement, but he was determined to get away from the monstrous creature that still stood just a few feet away.

"I'm sorry," he stammered, "I didn't... I didn't mean to disturb you."

The woman continued to stare at him for a moment longer, before slowly looking down at her own corpse.

"I shouldn't be here," Ben said. "I'll leave."

Realizing that she still seemed strangely calm, he took a deep breath before turning to walk away. Before he could take even a single step, however, he was shocked to see Mary – or, at least, the young woman he'd known as Mary – standing right behind him.

"I'm so sorry," she said calmly, with emotionless, glassy eyes. "I *did* tell you not to come down here."

CHAPTER TWENTY-ONE

"WHO ARE YOU?" he asked, disturbed by her preternatural change of disposition. "Your name isn't Mary Moore, is it?"

"Isn't it?" she replied.

"That's Mary Moore," he continued, turning and looking down for a moment at the corpse, then at the ghostly figure that remained a little further back in the shadows. After a moment, he turned to the girl again. "I read the letter," he continued. "She mentioned that she's in her fifties. You're not Mary. *She* is."

He waited, but she simply stared at him with a faint smile on her lips.

"Why did you lie?" he asked.

"Who says I lied?"

"I've read the letter!" he said firmly.

"There's no point maintaining this charade for even a moment longer. You're going to tell me what's going on, and you're going to tell me right now."

"Am I?"

"I'm a -"

"A police officer, yes," she said, interrupting him. "My word, how many times have you repeated that fact tonight? Twenty? Thirty? I understand, you're a man of the law, even if you're not a very *impressive* specimen."

"Who are you?" he asked again.

"I already told you," she replied, "I -"

"Don't lie to me!" he shouted, struggling to maintain his composure. "Don't you dare lie to me. You've been hiding something ever since I first came into this house, you've been playing me for a fool, but now you're going to tell me everything." He paused as he thought back to Lomax's final words. "He tried to warn me," he continued. "Why didn't I listen to him immediately?"

The girl opened her mouth to say something, but then she hesitated as the smile began to fade from her lips. After a moment, she peered past Ben, looking down toward the corpse on the floor. Now the tears were returning to her eyes, and finally she took a deep breath before muttering something under her breath.

"What did you say?" Ben asked.

She muttered the same thing, but again her

voice was too quiet. She seemed to be in shock.

"What did you say?" Ben asked again.

"I remember," she said finally. "It must be being down here, but... I remember."

He waited, but now she was in some kind of daze. It was as if all the memories were rushing back into her head, and now she was having trouble making sense of the truth about her own life.

"I was a good girl," she said after a moment, her voice trembling with emotion. "Not perfect, of course. Nobody is. But I was happy, and I was optimistic, and in my own way I suppose I was clever enough." Her voice briefly trailed off, as if she was lost in thought. "My biggest failing," she added eventually, "was that I believed wholeheartedly and blindly in the transformative power of love. I believed it was love that would define me, I believed it was only a matter of time before I met somebody who loved me truly and deeply. I don't think it ever occurred to me that anything else might happen."

"Why are you telling me this?" Ben asked. "I want to know who you are."

"When I grew up, I began to wonder how long I would have to wait. I reached marrying age, and nothing happened, and I got older and older while all the other girls in town began to pair off with local boys. I don't know what it was about me that was so repulsive, but evidently something put them all off me, until I started to consider the possibility that I would end up as a spinster. Eventually I began to accept my fate, but then...

Again, her voice trailed off.

"But then what?" Ben asked. "You're not too old to get married, not at all."

"Then *he* came into my life," she replied, still staring at the corpse. "Maurice Renshaw. I suppose I should have been suspicious, given the way that he swooped in and romanced me. Why would anyone be interested in someone like me? By that point, my parents had died and I was living here at Fenford Cottage on my own. I knew I was too old for courting, or at least I *thought* I was. I certainly wasn't entirely naive, of course, but gradually I let Maurice get under my skin, until I was certain that I had finally found the love I was craving. For six months, I was truly, genuinely happy."

"It was Mary who knew Maurice," Ben said, "unless... Did you *both* know him? How are you connected to this woman, and to this house?"

"When he left," she continued, "my heart was broken. He just abandoned me, as if suddenly I no longer mattered, as if I'd become some kind of joke to him. It was so pathetic, I should have been stronger than that, but I let the pain and hatred turn me into a monster. I lived all alone here, eking out a life from my inheritance, supplementing my income with some cleaning work in town. Always thinking about the life that could have been mine. If Maurice had just been true, and honest, I could have been happy. Instead, I stayed here and became..."

She paused, and slowly her gaze shifted. Instead of looking at the corpse on the floor, she was now looking directly at the ghostly woman.

"What's your name?" Ben asked.

"I already told you," she replied. "Mary."

"But *she* was Mary!" he said angrily, feeling as if she'd begun to treat him like an idiot.

"Yes," she said, "she was."

"Then how -"

"One house," she added, "haunted by two ghosts of the same woman."

Staring at her, Ben realized she was serious. He wanted to try to reason with her, but now he was worried about the true depths of her madness, and about what she might do if he tried to make her see sense. Again, he was consumed by the certain knowledge that he had to get out of the house, even if that meant trying again to find some way through the broken window.

"It's almost three in the morning," he pointed out, just about managing to hide the fear from his voice. "Everything will seem much better in the cold light of day, so let's just -"

"You don't get it, do you?" she snapped angrily.

"Mary -"

"She's me!" she continued. "I'm her! She's what I became! She hung herself, and now there are two of us haunting this house! She's the bitter, angry Mary who ended her own life, and I'm the young Mary who still had hope! We're the same person and now I can't ever get away from what I became!"

He stepped toward her and reached out to touch her arm, to prove to her – and to himself – that she was no ghost.

"Mary, I -"

Suddenly she put her hands against her face and screamed, and in that instant she faded from view, just as the ghostly figure had faded from view upstairs. Ben stumbled toward her, convinced that this had to be some trick of the light, but she was truly gone. A moment later he heard a slamming sound from upstairs, and he realized that it could only have come from the door at the top of the basement steps.

He ran back through the basement, desperate to get out. When he reached the top of the steps, however, he found that the door had been shut and bolted from the other side. He tried again and again to get it open, to no avail, and in the cramped space he soon found it hopeless to even try to break his way through.

"Mary!" he shouted, banging his fists against the wood. "You can't leave me down here!

Mary, open this door immediately!"

CHAPTER TWENTY-TWO

THE DOOR SHUDDERED IN its frame, but Ben quickly found that the hinges were too firmly attached. Having given up trying to break his way through using sheer force, and having failed to get the bolt loose, he'd resorted to a desperate attempt to pull the hinges away from the wood. Even this had failed, however, and he was starting to realize that there was no way out of the basement. At least, not through the door.

Stepping back, he listened to the silence.

"Mary," he said finally, even though he had no idea whether she could hear him, "please, listen to me. I only want to help you, but first I need you to let me out of here. What good does it do to trap me in the basement like this? I've been on your side from the start, and I want to help you work out what's really happening here."

He waited, imagining her standing on the other side of the door.

"Mary, I'm begging you," he continued. "Open the door so that I can help you fix this. There's no need to be scared. If you've got your memories back, then now's the perfect time for me to help you, but I can't do it from in here. Please, do the right thing."

He waited.

There was no answer.

Realizing that this course of action was hopeless, Ben turned and looked back down the stone steps. He hadn't seen any other way out of the basement while he was down there, but that didn't mean that one might not exist. He knew that he'd have to go back down and search for another set of stairs, or perhaps for a window set high in one of the walls, or even for a set of tools that might help him get the door open. The prospect filled him with dread, but at the same time he could think of no better idea.

For a moment, however, he thought of the dead woman. He tried to remind himself that ghosts didn't exist, yet now he'd seen enough to know that something very strange was happening in the house. Mary and the old woman had both disappeared before his eyes. Perhaps, he reasoned, they *were* ghosts.

Once he'd mustered enough courage, he made his way back down to the basement. He still had his torch, and he aimed the beam straight ahead as he hoped and prayed that the ghostly woman would not reappear. At least she'd seemed much calmer in the basement, whereas if anything it had been young Mary who had become frantic and angry. He still couldn't quite wrap his head around the idea of them both being ghosts of the same dead person, but he preferred to get out of the cottage now and ask questions later.

Reaching the basement's first room, he began to search for something that might aid his egress. He knew he was hoping for a miracle, but he couldn't lose hope, not yet. By the time he'd checked the entire room, however, he realized that he would have to go along the short corridor and into the other part of the basement. As he walked through, he told himself to push the fear from his mind, but sure enough a moment later he saw the corpse on the floor. Of the ghostly old woman, however, there was no sign.

He shone the torch's beam all around, and he saw that he was alone. At first, that felt like comfort, although he quickly realized that she might appear again at any moment, and from any direction.

As he started to search the room, he found himself continually looking over his shoulder, terrified that the old woman would come for him again. At the same time, he was starting to notice a faint sobbing sound that seemed to be coming from every direction at one. Initially he told himself that the sound was just in his head, that his mind was starting to crack under all the pressure, but after a couple of minutes he realized that somebody seemed to be sobbing in the far corner. Finally he turned and looked more closely, and he began to see the old woman kneeling just a few feet from her own corpse, sobbing into her hands.

He froze, too terrified to make a sound.

Still she sobbed, and Ben couldn't help but notice that she seemed much changed from before. He wanted to go back through to the other part of the basement, to try some other method of breaking through the door, so he slowly began to edge toward the corridor, hoping that he would draw no attention to himself.

"What did I become?" the old woman groaned suddenly.

Ben stopped.

The woman lowered her hands from her dead face, and now she stared at the corpse on the floor. There was no denying that the corpse *was* her, but after a moment Ben began to notice certain other features of her face that seemed familiar. Again, he told himself at first that he had to be wrong, but he was starting to see similarities between the old woman and Mary, as if perhaps they might be the same person after all. He told himself that this was impossible, that he was imagining things, but the resemblance was becoming more and more clear.

"Mary?" he said finally.

Slowly, she turned to look at him. Her face was still so old and dead, but with each passing second he was increasingly sure that it *was* her.

"How?" he asked. "I mean... how can one person have two ghosts? Even if ghosts were real..."

"I was so young and innocent back then," she replied, her voice sounding weathered and harsh. "I had no idea of the harsh life that lay ahead of me. Of the evil that would befall me. Of the cruelty."

Backing against the wall, Ben prepared to make a run for the stairs.

"He left me here to rot," the older Mary snarled. "He twisted my heart until it was blackened. You ask how there can be two ghosts of me? Perhaps it's because, by the end of my life, I felt like someone else entirely. I haunt this house, and my younger self haunts me."

"No," Ben replied, "that's not possible."

"Maurice cared nothing for me," she continued. "He pretended to love me, but then he walked away and never looked back. He was going to take me to London, but then he never contacted me again. How could I ever have any faith in humanity after that?"

"Belgravia," Ben stammered.

"That's where he lived," she replied mournfully. "He was going to open the house up, and then send for me. But he never sent for me."

"He called," Ben said. "He's called so many times over the years. You don't have a telephone here, but he called the station. The house is empty, but a man called from Belgravia and asked us to come and check on you."

"Liar!" she snapped.

"That means he must have cared," Ben continued. "I don't know why he didn't come back all those years ago, but he didn't forget you. Someone has been calling the station for decades, it must have been him!"

"Why are you saying these things?" she asked, slowly starting to get to her feet.

"Because it's true!" he told her. "I can't claim to know exactly what happened, but I assure you that someone from a house in Belgravia -"

"Liar!" she shouted angrily, her face twisting to become a vision of pain and fury. "Don't you dare try to defend him!"

"I'm just telling you what happened!" he replied, as he began to edge toward the corridor. "If it wasn't him, then who was it? Someone used a telephone to call from an abandoned house in

Belgravia, over and over again, asking someone to come out here and check on you. Someone wanted to know that you're alright. Someone cared. If it wasn't this Maurice Renshaw man, then who else could it have been?"

"You're just as bad as him," she sneered.

"I swear, Maurice telephoned. I think... I think, whatever happened, he still cared. He was -"

"Liar!" she screamed, suddenly lunging at him.

Turning, Ben races along the corridor, desperately trying to get to the stairs. He slammed into one of the walls, but he soon made it all the way up the stairs, throwing himself against the door. Still finding it locked, he began pulling furiously on the door in an attempt to find some way out.

"Help!" he shouted, banging his fists against the wood. "You have to get me out of here! She -"

Before he could finish, he heard a rustling sound. Looking down the stone steps, he saw to his horror that the ghostly old woman was now slowly making her way up toward him. Her eyes were filled with pure hatred, and she began to raise her hands as if she was preparing to wrap them around his throat.

"Help me!" he yelled, banging against the door again. "Please! Open this door immediately!"

.

CHAPTER TWENTY-THREE

SUDDENLY THE DOOR CLICKED and swung open. Ben fell through, landing in a breathless heap on the floor, and then he was dragged out of the way before the door slammed shut.

Gasping, Ben rolled onto his back and look up to see the younger version of Mary staring down at him.

"You don't belong to her," she said calmly. "You belong to me."

"What?" he stammered.

"She's scared of me now," she continued. "It took me a long time to realize who I am. Now that I know, I'm in control. This is *my* house, so we're going to play by my rules."

Sitting up, Ben felt a twinge of pain in his ribs. He hesitated, then he tried to get to his feet, only to find that the pain intensified. As he waited a moment and tried to get his breath back, he became very much aware of the girl standing nearby and simply watching him. When he finally looked up at her, he was shocked by the sight of a smile on her lips.

"I did nothing," she said after a moment, "to deserve ending up like that monster. I was good, I did everything right, so why did I turn into that *thing*? Why did my life end, after fifty-seven years, with me putting a noose around my neck and hanging myself in the basement? And did you read the note that I wrote? So pathetic. So worthless. Did I really let my life fade away, all because of that Maurice Renshaw man?"

"I can help you," he replied, "but first -"

"I don't need your help," she said firmly. "Not now that I know who I am. Still, there's only room for one ghost around here, and I think it's obvious who that should be."

Turning, Ben tried again to get to his feet, and then he began to crawl toward the front room. He could just about see the broken window, and he told himself that this time he wasn't going to let anything hold him back. Even if all those terrible thoughts and emotions came rushing into his head again, he was determined to haul himself out into the garden, and then to get to the patrol car. Even as he dragged himself past Lomax's corpse, he told himself that he wasn't going to let anything stop him.

Suddenly a foot pressed down hard on the small of his back, pushing him against the floor, and he heard Mary laugh.

"You should have walked away tonight," she told him after a moment. "You could be safely tucked up in bed by now, and none of this would have happened, but you had to come inside and try to be a hero. What's the lesson of that particular story, then? That people should keep to themselves? That no good comes of mixing? I think that makes sense. After all, if I'd never met Maurice, I'd have stayed as I am now instead of turning into that ghoulish old hag at the end of my pathetic, miserable life."

She pushed harder, causing Ben to let out a gasp of pain.

"I've been haunting this house for almost a hundred years," she continued. "Can you imagine what that's like? For nearly a century, I was running around terrified, not knowing what was happening. I should thank you for luring me into the basement. Without you, I might have been like that forever. Now I can really push the limits." Crouching down, she placed a knee against Ben's back. "Anyone who comes into this house deserves to suffer," she added. "I suffered a miserable death in here. Why shouldn't everyone else?"

"Please," Ben gasped, trying desperately to push her away but finding that he was too weak. "Stop..."

"How many of you do you think there'll be after you die?" she asked. "Do you think you'll have two ghosts, or will you just have one, like all the other boring people? Maybe I'm the only one who was so interesting, so brilliant, that she produced two."

"Mary..."

"Yes, that's my name," she said brightly. "You're not very good at begging, are you?"

"Please... you don't have to do this..."

"Such a goody two shoes," she purred, as the basement door once again creaked open behind her. "And what's that noise? Could it be that the other me has decided to show her face?"

Turning, Ben saw that the ghostly old woman had reached the top of the stairs, although now she was holding back, almost as if she was scared of her younger self. A moment later she took a tentative step forward.

"What do you want?" the younger Mary asked scornfully, turning to her. "You belong in the basement now, next to our wretched corpse. Don't think I haven't noticed that you're the reason we're dead to begin with. I was a bright, smart child. *You're* the one who ruined everything when I got older!"

The older Mary lowered her head, as if she felt ashamed.

"Leave!" the younger girl screamed suddenly, getting to her feet and storming toward the other woman. "Go! Now! Back to the basement!"

The older Mary turned and faded from view, leaving her younger version to slam the basement door shut.

"She needs to know her place," she muttered angrily. "I'm going to teach her a lesson before I banish her forever."

Ignoring those words, Ben focused on dragging himself through to the front room. His progress was painfully slow, but soon he was at the window, and once again he felt somebody else's emotions rushing into his mind. There was no anger this time, however, as instead he felt a kind of sorrow and dread, maybe even guilt. As he reached up toward the window with a trembling hand, he felt true misery starting to wash through his soul.

Finally, unable to lift himself up from the floor, he turned and slumped against the wall. Looking back across the room, he saw the younger Mary standing in the doorway, watching him with wry amusement.

"You don't have to do any of this," he told her. "You said it yourself, when you were young you -"

"I don't need a lecture," she snapped.

"But you told me you were a good person," he continued. "That's the whole reason why you split into two ghosts, isn't it? Because the younger version of you was so completely different to the older version." He paused, and now he felt as if he was getting through to her. "You're the ghost of Mary Moore's best side. Her true side. You're the ghost of the woman she was *before* her life went wrong. Do you really want to turn into the other version of yourself? Do you really want to become that thing in the basement?"

"Maybe I don't have a choice," she said darkly.

"Or maybe you do," he pointed out.

"I'm dead," she replied. "I think it's too late for me to make big life choices."

"It's never too late," he told her. "Not for anyone. You don't have to become that -"

"Monster?"

"You don't have to become her," he continued. "Really, you don't. You never did. I'm sorry for everything that happened to you while you were alive, but even now you don't have to become that thing in the basement. Until you remembered everything, you were brave and smart, I think you even saved my life. Don't let go of all that now. Let me go and I'll do whatever I can to help you, I'll find out what happened to Maurice Renshaw. I won't let you down, I promise."

"You don't mean that," she replied, and now there were fresh tears in her eyes.

"You have my word," he told her. "As a man, and as -"

"An officer of the law?" She paused, and then a faint smile reached her lips. "I think you mentioned once that you were one of those."

"Let me help you."

She hesitated, before stepping closer to him and then kneeling down. She seemed lost in thought, but finally her smile grew slightly. Staring at Ben for a moment, she opened her mouth to say something but then she hesitated.

"See?" he said finally. "Nothing in this whole world say that you have to become that creature in the basement."

"Maybe you're right," she replied, and then slowly she reached a hand out toward his face. For a few seconds, it seemed that she was going to touch his cheek, but then her smile slipped and she tore the police badge from his shirt before slashing it against his face. "But maybe I *want* to become her!"

CHAPTER TWENTY-FOUR

GASPING, BEN TURNED AWAY as he felt blood dribbling from the gash on his cheek. A moment later he turned back just in time to see Mary tossing the badge aside, and then she grabbed his throat and squeezed tight.

"I'm afraid your well-intentioned words didn't have any impact," she snarled. "Everyone who sets foot in this house is going to experience my pain. I can pour it into your head, you know. The older me used it to stop you getting out through the window, but *I* think you need to live with it until you die."

Grinning, she leaned closer to him, until her dead eyes seemed to be boring into his soul.

"I was screwed over from birth," she continued, "I just didn't know it. I was always destined to become that old bitch in the basement, I was always doomed to end up hanging myself and leaving some pathetic note behind. I could no more change my fate, than I could change my face. That's who I was always going to be, my whole life was set out from beginning to end, so I might as well accept that fact."

"You had a choice!" Ben gurgled, as Mary's hand tightened against his throat. "You still do!"

"Once she and I are the same, there'll be no need for two of us," she explained. "That's my theory, anyway. We'll become one ghost, the only ghost there ever should have been. And anyone who comes here will feel my wrath!"

Trying to push her away, Ben nevertheless felt himself getting weaker and weaker. He puts his hands on her shoulders and tried desperately to force her back, but she was laughing now and he felt as if all the strength was draining from his body. The pain in his ribs was becoming stronger, and he found that he couldn't force himself to rise up and try to get out through the window. Instead, he could only feel Mary's grip tightening with each passing second, choking the life from him.

"You don't have to do this..." Ben gasped breathlessly.

Mary smiled.

And then, just as she tightened her grip on his throat, she screamed as the older Mary leaned straight through her from behind. An older face burst out from the younger face, staring straight at Ben as the grip around his throat loosened.

"Go!" the older Mary snarled, before pulling back and dragging her younger form with her.

"No!" the girl screamed, but already she was being held down.

"Go!" the older ghost shouted again. "Leave my home!"

"I -"

"Is it true?" she continued. "Did Maurice really ask you to come and check on me?"

"Yes," he stammered, "but -"

"Then go!" she yelled. "Now!"

For a moment, Ben could only stare in horror as the two women struggled. The younger Mary was trying every possible way to get free, and slowly the pair of them began to merge. It was as if their bodies were blurring together, as if they were fighting for supremacy as they continued to combine. At first, the sight was horrific, as two entirely distinct bodies twisted and writhed, but gradually Ben began to notice that their hands seemed to be binding together. Soon it was only the faces that seemed truly separate, with both the younger and older forms of Mary still vying to become the one true ghost of the woman who had lived all her life at Fenford Cottage.

Finally, just as the younger face seemed to

be gaining dominance, the older face broke free for a moment and screamed at Ben again.

"Go!"

Dragging himself up, he found that his mind was no longer filled with strange emotions as he hauled himself through the window. He pushed against the pain and toppled over the edge, landing hard on the ground outside, and then he turned and began to pull himself along the path. The night air was still icy, and he could hear more and more screams coming from over his shoulder, but it wasn't until he reached the gate that he dared to look over his shoulder.

The cottage remained dark, of course, just as it had been when he'd first arrived. Through the broken window, however, he briefly saw the two ghostly figures as they struggled against one another. And then, just as the terrible battle seemed set to rage forever, a scream rang out and both ghosts disappeared into the darkness.

Ben pulled the gate open and crawled out onto the side of the road, convinced that leaving the threshold of the property would confer some extra safety, and then he looked at the cottage again and waited.

All was silent now.

All was calm.

He waited, convinced that this couldn't be the end of it, that one or other of the ghosts would surely appear again. When this had still not happened even after a few more minutes had passed, he pushed through the pain and hauled himself up, leaning against the edge of the wall. He couldn't help watching the cottage, and after a few seconds he began to consider going back inside. He wanted to know for certain what had happened, but in the end something held him back. The house looked so still and quiet now, and he truly preferred not to interfere. He could only hope that this meant that peace had come to the ghost of Fenford Cottage.

On the drive back to town, he tried to work out what he was going to tell people. There was no chance of covering matters up, since Inspector Lomax's body remained in the cottage and would have to be retrieved in the morning. At the same time, he knew that he would be dismissed as a madman if he tried to tell anyone about the ghost, or ghosts, of Mary Moore. Would it be possible to come up with some kind of halfway point, some version of the truth that omitted the supernatural elements? This seemed unlikely, so he told himself that he would simply have to tell the truth as he had experienced it, and then he would have to hope for understanding. Mary's body would have to be removed from the basement, and she would have to be given a proper burial. And then, finally, Fenford Cottage might become peaceful again.

As soon as he reached the police station, he hurried out of the car and made his way inside. Still rehearsing what he was going to say, he entered the main office and opened his mouth to speak, before realizing that he was alone. With Lomax gone, there were only a couple of other sergeants in the town, and they were all at home.

Feeling exhausted, Ben headed to the desk and slumped down. There was nothing else for it, he told himself; he would have to wait a few more hours until morning, and then someone else would arrive to open the station.

He sat in silence, and slowly his eyes began to close.

Suddenly the the telephone rang, jolting him out of what was about to become a deep sleep. Startled by the loud noise, he stared for a moment before lifting the receiver. Already, he worried that he would hear the same voice on the other end of the line, the voice that he'd heard at the start of the night.

It ended – as it had begun – with a phone call late at night.

He waited.

Silence.

"Hello?" he said finally. "Bilside Police Station, Sergeant Warner speaking, how can I -"

"You have to go and check on her," the voice snapped, and indeed it was the same voice that he'd heard earlier. "I need you to make a... what do they call it? A welfare check! I need you to make a welfare check on Mary Moore at Fenford Cottage. Please, it's urgent, I think something might be terribly wrong!"

"I've been out there," Ben said, his voice sounding bare and fragile.

"Oh, it's terrible," the voice continued, interrupting again. "Something's wrong, I know it. Please, for the love of all that's holy, you have to go and see that she's -"

Suddenly the voice stopped.

"You've been?" it added finally.

"I went to Fenford Cottage tonight," Ben explained, "and I did in fact see Miss Mary Moore."

"How is she?" the voice asked. "I feel so awful. I was supposed to send for her, but when I got to London I... I don't know exactly what happened, except that I was crossing the street and a carriage hit me. After that, I woke up here at home, and I haven't been able to leave since. I haven't been able to get word to her. Please, you must tell me, how is she?"

Ben opened his mouth to answer, but then he felt something sharp digging into the side of his chest. Reaching into his pocket, he was surprised when he pulled out his police badge. One edge was caked in blood, from where it had been slashed across his face. Young Mary had tossed it aside, and in the confusion he'd not managed to retrieve it, yet somehow – in the end – it had been placed safely in his pocket.

"Please," the voice on the phone begged, "tell me. Is she okay?"

"I think perhaps she is," Ben replied. "I think she might be at peace with herself. After all these years."

MARY

Also by Amy Cross

The Haunting of Lannister Hall

For many years, no living soul has set foot in Lannister Hall. High fences surround the property, and guards work 24/7 to make sure that nobody breaks through. Finally, however, something has changed. Finally permission has been granted to a small team who are going to go into the house and uncover its darkest secrets.

Lannister Hall was once the scene of tragedy. Catherine Lannister was found dead, and both her husband and child were never seen again. It's said that Catherine's ghost still walks the empty rooms, searching for her daughter. But when three investigators arrive at the house, how will the ghost react? Will she welcome their help, or will she turn on them as they attempt to get to the truth?

The Haunting of Lannister Hall is a ghost story about a haunted house, about a woman who will do anything for her daughter, and about a deadly warning once given by a dying mother.

Also by Amy Cross

The Strangler's Daughter

Lisa Ashford's father is a murderer. Ten years ago, he strangled several women, but he was never caught by the police. He eventually promised his daughter that it would never happen again, and their lives seemed to go back to normal. But now there's another body...

Timid and shy, Lisa struggles to make sense of the world. Everyone tells her that she's different, that she's a little slow in the head. Last time her father killed, she was an impressionable young girl who believed all his excuses. Having just lost her mother, she was terrified of being left all alone.

Now, however, Lisa's a young woman, and ignoring the truth isn't so easy. Can she still stand by while her father commits terrible crimes? Or will she take a stand and try to stop him? Is he even telling the truth about why he kills? And if she finally disobeys his instructions, how far will he go in order to keep his deadly secrets? Could Lisa be his next victim?

Also by Amy Cross

**Ten Chimes to Midnight:
A Collection of Ghost Stories**

A train pulls into an abandoned station late at night. But what's waiting, out on the platform, for the passengers?

A woman returns to her childhood home, seeking revenge against the spirit that killed her entire family. But will she be given the chance?

An angry husband confronts a faded old magician. Is he about to learn a startling secret about the nature of life and death?

Ten Chimes to Midnight is a collection, featuring the brand new stories By the Time You Finish Reading This Short Story..., The Carriage, Probate, The Sleeping Ghost, Bill, The Ghost of Pentarth Asylum, The B*tch and the B*stard and As I Put My Card Back in the Deck..., as well as new versions of The Legend of Bug-Eyed Pete and the 2014 novella Hugo: The Lockton Downs Haunting.

Also by Amy Cross

The Devil, the Witch and the Whore
(The Deal book 1)

"Leave the forest alone. Whatever's out there, just let it be. Don't make it angry."

When a horrific discovery is made at the edge of town, Sheriff James Kopperud realizes the answers he seeks might be waiting beyond in the vast forest. But everybody in the town of Deal knows that there's something out there in the forest, something that should never be disturbed. A deal was made long ago, a deal that was supposed to keep the town safe. And if he insists on investigating the murder of a local girl, James is going to have to break that deal and head out into the wilderness.

Meanwhile, James has no idea that his estranged daughter Ramsey has returned to town. Ramsey is running from something, and she thinks she can find safety in the vast tunnel system that runs beneath the forest. Before long, however, Ramsey finds herself coming face to face with creatures that hide in the shadows. One of these creatures is known as the devil, and another is known as the witch. They're both waiting for the whore to arrive, but for very different reasons. And soon Ramsey is offered a terrible deal, one that could save or destroy the entire town, and maybe even the world.

Also by Amy Cross

The Soul Auction

"I saw a woman on the beach. I watched her face a demon."

Thirty years after her mother's death, Alice Ashcroft is drawn back to the coastal English town of Curridge. Somebody in Curridge has been reviewing Alice's novels online, and in those reviews there have been tantalizing hints at a hidden truth. A truth that seems to be linked to her dead mother.

"Thirty years ago, there was a soul auction."

Once she reaches Curridge, Alice finds strange things happening all around her. Something attacks her car. A figure watches her on the beach at night. And when she tries to find the person who has been reviewing her books, she makes a horrific discovery.

What really happened to Alice's mother thirty years ago? Who was she talking to, just moments before dropping dead on the beach? What caused a huge rockfall that nearly tore a nearby cliff-face in half? And what sinister presence is lurking in the grounds of the local church?

Also by Amy Cross

Darper Danver: The Complete First Series

Five years ago, three friends went to a remote cabin in the woods and tried to contact the spirit of a long-dead soldier. They thought they could control whatever happened next. They were wrong...

Newly released from prison, Cassie Briggs returns to Fort Powell, determined to get her life back on track. Soon, however, she begins to suspect that an ancient evil still lurks in the nearby cabin. Was the mysterious Darper Danver really destroyed all those years ago, or does her spirit still linger, waiting for a chance to return?

As Cassie and her ex-boyfriend Fisher are finally forced to face the truth about what happened in the cabin, they realize that Darper isn't ready to let go of their lives just yet. Meanwhile, a vengeful woman plots revenge for her brother's murder, and a New York ghost writer arrives in town to uncover the truth. Before long, strange carvings begin to appear around town and blood starts to flow once again.

Also by Amy Cross

The Ghost of Molly Holt

"Molly Holt is dead. There's nothing to fear in this house."

When three teenagers set out to explore an abandoned house in the middle of a forest, they think they've found the location where the infamous Molly Holt video was filmed.

They've found much more than that...

Tim doesn't believe in ghosts, but he has a crush on a girl who does. That's why he ends up taking her out to the house, and it's also why he lets her take his only flashlight. But as they explore the house together, Tim and Becky start to realize that something else might be lurking in the shadows.

Something that, ten years ago, suffered unimaginable pain.

Something that won't rest until a terrible wrong has been put right.

Also by Amy Cross

American Coven

He kidnapped three women and held them in his basement. He thought they couldn't fight back. He was wrong...

Snatched from the street near her home, Holly Carter is taken to a rural house and thrown down into a stone basement. She meets two other women who have also been kidnapped, and soon Holly learns about the horrific rituals that take place in the house. Eventually, she's called upstairs to take her place in the ice bath.

As her nightmare continues, however, Holly learns about a mysterious power that exists in the basement, and which the three women might be able to harness. When they finally manage to get through the metal door, however, the women have no idea that their fight for freedom is going to stretch out for more than a decade, or that it will culminate in a final, devastating demonstration of their new-found powers.

Also by Amy Cross

The Ash House

Why would anyone ever return to a haunted house?

For Diane Mercer the answer is simple. She's dying of cancer, and she wants to know once and for all whether ghosts are real.

Heading home with her young son, Diane is determined to find out whether the stories are real. After all, everyone else claimed to see and hear strange things in the house over the years. Everyone except Diane had some kind of experience in the house, or in the little ash house in the yard.

As Diane explores the house where she grew up, however, her son is exploring the yard and the forest. And while his mother might be struggling to come to terms with her own impending death, Daniel Mercer is puzzled by fleeting appearances of a strange little girl who seems drawn to the ash house, and by strange, rasping coughs that he keeps hearing at night.

The Ash House is a horror novel about a woman who desperately wants to know what will happen to her when she dies, and about a boy who uncovers the shocking truth about a young girl's murder.

Also by Amy Cross

Haunted

Twenty years ago, the ghost of a dead little girl drove Sheriff Michael Blaine to his death.

Now, that same ghost is coming for his daughter.

Returning to the small town where she grew up, Alex Roberts is determined to live a normal, quiet life. For the residents of Railham, however, she's an unwelcome reminder of the town's darkest hour.

Twenty years ago, nine-year-old Mo Garvey was found brutally murdered in a nearby forest. Everyone thinks that Alex's father was responsible, but if the killer was brought to justice, why is the ghost of Mo Garvey still after revenge?

And how far will the real killer go to protect his secret, when Alex starts getting closer to the truth?

Haunted is a horror novel about a woman who has to face her past, about a town that would rather forget, and about a little girl who refuses to let death stand in her way.

AMY CROSS

Also by Amy Cross

The Curse of Wetherley House

"If you walk through that door, Evil Mary will get you."

When she agrees to visit a supposedly haunted house with an old friend, Rosie assumes she'll encounter nothing more scary than a few creaks and bumps in the night. Even the legend of Evil Mary doesn't put her off. After all, she knows ghosts aren't real. But when Mary makes her first appearance, Rosie realizes she might already be trapped.

For more than a century, Wetherley House has been cursed. A horrific encounter on a remote road in the late 1800's has already caused a chain of misery and pain for all those who live at the house. Wetherley House was abandoned long ago, after a terrible discovery in the basement, something has remained undetected within its room. And even the local children know that Evil Mary waits in the house for anyone foolish enough to walk through the front door.

Before long, Rosie realizes that her entire life has been defined by the spirit of a woman who died in agony. Can she become the first person to escape Evil Mary, or will she fall victim to the same fate as the house's other occupants?

AMY CROSS

Also by Amy Cross

The Ghosts of Hexley Airport

Ten years ago, more than two hundred people died in a horrific plane crash at Hexley Airport.

Today, some say their ghosts still haunt the terminal building.

When she starts her new job at the airport, working a night shift as part of the security team, Casey assumes the stories about the place can't be true. Even when she has a strange encounter in a deserted part of the departure hall, she's certain that ghosts aren't real.

Soon, however, she's forced to face the truth. Not only is there something haunting the airport's buildings and tarmac, but a sinister force is working behind the scenes to replicate the circumstances of the original accident. And as a snowstorm moves in, Hexley Airport looks set to witness yet another disaster.

AMY CROSS

Also by Amy Cross

The Girl Who Never Came Back

Twenty years ago, Charlotte Abernathy vanished while playing near her family's house. Despite a frantic search, no trace of her was found until a year later, when the little girl turned up on the doorstep with no memory of where she'd been.

Today, Charlotte has put her mysterious ordeal behind her, even though she's never learned where she was during that missing year. However, when her eight-year-old niece vanishes in similar circumstances, a fully-grown Charlotte is forced to make a fresh attempt to uncover the truth.

Originally published in 2013, the fully revised and updated version of *The Girl Who Never Came Back* tells the harrowing story of a woman who thought she could forget her past, and of a little girl caught in the tangled web of a dark family secret.

Also by Amy Cross

Asylum
(The Asylum Trilogy book 1)

"No-one ever leaves Lakehurst. The staff, the patients, the ghosts... Once you're here, you're stuck forever."

After shooting her little brother dead, Annie Radford is sent to Lakehurst psychiatric hospital for assessment. Hearing voices in her head, Annie is forced to undergo experimental new treatments devised by a mysterious old man who lives in the hospital's attic. It soon becomes clear that the hospital's staff, led by the vicious Nurse Winter, are hiding something horrific at Lakehurst.

As Annie struggles to survive the hospital, she learns more about Nurse Winter's own story. Once a promising young medical student, Kirsten Winter also heard voices in her head. Voices that traveled a long way to reach her. Voices that have a plan of their own. Voices that will stop at nothing to get what they want.

What kind of signals are being transmitted from the basement of the hospital? Who is the old man in the attic? Why are living human brains kept in jars? And what is the dark secret that lurks at the heart of the hospital?

AMY CROSS

BOOKS BY AMY CROSS

For more information, visit:

www. amycross.com

AMY CROSS

Printed in Great Britain
by Amazon